"Did you know that each room comes with an armoire stocked with sex toys?"

Okay, so Mia wasn't quite as innocent as her image would suggest. An armoire stocked with sex toys? Bax would like to see those. See her. Touch— Damn it. "How does that work?" he asked, hoping she hadn't noticed his voice crack.

She unsuccessfully hid a snicker. "That would depend on the guest."

She was killing him here. Because she could. Because she knew he was getting hard at her matter-of-fact voice, at that wicked smile. He cleared his throat. "No, I mean those kinds of amenities really couldn't be reused, could they?"

"It depends. Anything that has the possibility of close contact is replaced for each guest. You should come down sometime and see the operation. You'd be impressed."

"I'm sure I would," he said, desperate to change the subject. Thankfully dinner arrived, and Bax threw himself into eating his pastrami on rye. It wasn't quite as effective as a cold shower, but as long as Mia didn't talk about sex toys anymore, he should be okay

He was kidding himself....

Blaze™

Dear Reader,

Welcome back to Hush!

It's been a while since we checked in to the gorgeous and sexy Hush hotel. So many of you have written asking to revisit the DO NOT DISTURB series that I couldn't resist a comeback. Only this time, there's a movie company in residence at the hotel, and concierge Mia Traverse not only discovers the body, but uses her smarts to find out who's behind the murder. Bax Milligan, the homicide detective assigned to the case, isn't crazy about Mia's "help," but he is crazy about her. Together they become a formidable team, both on the job and in the bedroom.

This was a particularly fun book for me. Since I used to work in the movie business and got to travel to exotic locations, I had a wonderful time remembering the sights, sounds and crazy personalities from those exciting days. Are some of the characters based on real celebrities I knew? I'll never tell.

Come join Mia and Bax and take a vacation where mystery and murder mix with glamour and romance at the one and only Hush hotel!

Love,

Jo Leigh

P.S. Look for my next DO NOT DISTURB book, *Have Mercy* in May 2008! And in June 2008 check out my linked story "Biting the Apple" in *Destination: Marriage.*

JO LEIGH
Coming Soon

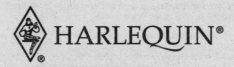

TORONTO • NEW YORK • LONDON
AMSTERDAM • PARIS • SYDNEY • HAMBURG
STOCKHOLM • ATHENS • TOKYO • MILAN • MADRID
PRAGUE • WARSAW • BUDAPEST • AUCKLAND

ISBN-13: 978-0-373-79390-7
ISBN-10:   0-373-79390-1

COMING SOON

www.eHarlequin.com

Printed in U.S.A.

ABOUT THE AUTHOR

Jo Leigh has written more than thirty novels for Harlequin and Silhouette Books since 1994. She's a triple RITA® Award finalist, most recently receiving a nomination from the Romance Writers of America for her Harlequin Blaze novel *Relentless*. She also teaches writing in workshops across the country.

Jo lives in Utah with her wonderful husband and their cute puppy, Jessie. You can come chat with her at her Web site, www.joleigh.com, and don't forget to check out her daily blog!

Books by Jo Leigh
HARLEQUIN BLAZE

2—GOING FOR IT!
23—SCENT OF A WOMAN
34—SENSUAL SECRETS
72—A DASH OF TEMPTATION
88—TRUTH OR DARE
122—ARM CANDY
134—THE ONE WHO GOT AWAY
165—A LICK AND A PROMISE
178—HUSH†
227—MINUTE BY MINUTE

265—CLOSER...
289—RELENTLESS*
301—RELEASE*
313—RECKONING*
345—KIDNAPPED††

†Do Not Distrub
*In Too Deep...
††Forbidden Fantasies

To my friend Debbi.
She knows why.

1

IT WAS JUST A MATTER of keeping her cool.

Mia could deal with movie stars. After all, she was a concierge at Hush, which was one of the most glamorous hotels in Manhattan, so she met major celebrities all the time. She could deal with the press. Again, thanks to Hush, especially because owner Piper Devon was so hands-on about her hotel, and the paparazzi never got tired of the beautiful heiress. And she could deal with the cranky Belgians on the fifth floor who wanted everything New York had to offer without paying for a thing.

The trick was handling all three at once.

Mia straightened her small gold name badge, her *Clefs d'Or* pin, then her skinny black tuxedo skirt as she adjusted her mental attitude and her smile. "Of course, Mr. Weinberg. I'll be sure to let housekeeping know you would prefer eiderdown pillows. They'll be ready for you by six o'clock."

Mr. Weinberg of the infamous Weinberg Film Company looked at Mia as if she were more distasteful than his pillows and strode off, trailed by a posse of assistants, most of them talking away on their Bluetooth headgear.

Mia turned immediately to Bobbi Tamony, the star of *Coming Soon*. She was dressed in a spectacularly sparkly gown that had protective paper all around the bodice, slippers on her feet, and her hair, world-famous in all the tabloids, rolled in giant curlers.

"Listen, sweetie, I have to be on set in two seconds, so could you make sure there's a limo waiting for me around ten tonight? I should be done by then and I want to get the hell out of here."

"No problem, Ms. Tamony. It will be waiting at the back entrance when you're ready to go."

"Thanks, hon," Bobbi said, waving her hand distractedly as she walked toward the front entrance.

It would have been nice to find a moment to breathe, but one of the Belgians moved from in front of the long, black lacquered reservation desk to her station at the far end. "We wish tickets for a big Broadway show, *si vous ne vous occupez pas.*"

"Of course, Monsieur Michaud. Would you like to see a list of the shows that are currently available?" Mia responded in French.

He nodded, then glanced around the lobby. "When will these movie people leave? So much noise," he said. "Very annoying."

"I'm afraid they'll be here for the rest of your stay. They've reserved their rooms for the entire month of June."

He snorted as Mia gave him a printout of the most popular shows. Not all of them, actually. Just the ones she could get tickets for.

He perused the list for several moments and Mia took advantage of the tiny break to quietly jot down notes about the pillows and the limo.

"This one." Michaud pointed to one of the long-running shows that rarely sold out on the weeknights.

"Is this for tonight?" she asked, holding back a sigh

when he nodded. It was already three-thirty. She'd started her shift at eight that morning, so he could have come at any time, but no. The only minute for certain guests was the last minute.

It took some time to get all the details taken care of, but Monsieur Michaud left on a bright note with the tickets and finally, Mia could relax.

Well, this was the job. She'd fought hard to get here. It had helped that she'd been raised all over the world in the best of the best hotels, that both her parents were concierges, and that she spoke five languages, including French. Still, getting this job at Hush when she was only twenty-eight... Unbelievable. Most concierges didn't even aspire to this level of hotel until they'd been on the job for at least fifteen years.

Maybe it had to do with how special Hush was, and the clientele the hotel catered to. In less dignified quarters, Hush was known as the sex hotel, but those more sophisticated understood that Hush was a haven of sensuality and luxury. A celebration of the mind, the spirit and most definitely the body.

She'd yet to meet a guest who hadn't left with a dreamy smile and a confident walk. Although these wacky movie people might be the first.

She got on the phone with the transportation department and set up Bobbi Tamony's limo with a driver she knew personally, then with Theresa, the housekeeping manager, to secure Weinberg's pillows, at least six from different suppliers. Neither of them had to mention that the Hush house pillows were some of the finest in the world. Everyone who stayed at Hush, at least the ones who thought they were Very Important People, had their own litmus tests for just how important they were. Sometimes it was the turndown service: the shades exactly three-quarters drawn, Godiva chocolates on the end table. Often it had to do with the liquor, particularly the champagne. Today it was pillows.

She answered a dozen successive calls, each of them sending her to her computer where she was plugged into a very exclusive and private Web site connecting concierges from every major hotel in the world. If she couldn't get her hands on something, one of her compatriots would, and eventually, all was well.

One thing about her job—the day certainly sped by. She hadn't been able to break away today, not even for lunch, which meant she'd missed her opportunity to sneak down to Exhibit A, the nightclub in Hush's basement, and watch the filming. But the movie company would be here for the rest of the month. In fact tonight her friends Carlane, an assistant concierge at the Helmsley and Jenna, a concierge at the Algonquin, were coming to meet her for dinner, followed by drinks at Erotique, the Hush bar.

It wasn't kosher to spend much time there, at least for her, but they were dying to see Danny Austen, the star of the film. In all likelihood they'd get their chance. He was something of a lush and a major flirt, but he was sweet and he hadn't been too, too demanding.

A ruckus at the restaurant had her leaning over her desk to see, but it was only the paparazzi. Or one paparazzo. Gerry Geiger. Trying yet again to gain access to the hotel. Piper had hired extra security to deal with the photographers and for the most part it had gone well. Except for Gerry. He was the trickiest son-of-a-gun of them all. The new security guys were on the spot, and with a minimum of fuss, things were back to normal. Well, as normal as Hush hotel ever got.

Back online she grinned when she read a plea from the Vegas Hard Rock Hotel concierge, hoping someone knew how to get six bat hearts. Bat hearts had to be available somewhere, and she was going to do her best to find them. Find them first.

It was exactly the type of game she liked best. When most people thought of a concierge, they thought of service. But for Mia, it was all about the hunt. The more impossible the request, the more she was in her element.

She sighed happily as she set to the task. It was yet another day in paradise.

DETECTIVE BAX MILLIGAN was in hell.

Not just because his regular partner was in the hospital with a broken pelvis, but the mook had hurt himself washing his car, and he'd managed to do it before he'd done any of the paperwork on the Fitzgerald murder.

Bax took another sip of coffee, sighed miserably, then got back to it. Page after page of cop speak about a case that wasn't getting solved anytime soon. Damn it to hell, too many cases weren't getting solved and that was the only part of the damn job he liked.

He kept writing words no regular human would ever say, careful not to miss a comma because nowadays it was more about procedure and protocol than catching the bad guys.

Well, he'd had it. Three months from now, marked with bold Xs on his desk calendar, he was outta here. He was moving to Colorado—Boulder to be precise. At the ripe old age of thirty-six, he was going back to school to finish his master's, and maybe get his Ph.D. The long-term plan was to teach and write, the emphasis on writing. He'd find himself a nice little college and talk about books, all kinds, read until he couldn't turn another page. In Boulder, he'd have friends who didn't give him shit about his books. Who didn't think he was a pussy for talking about Dickens. Three more months filled with death and gangs and god-damned paperwork.

He'd even lined up a part-time job at the university library. Not a lot of money, but he'd been socking away his pennies for a hell of a long time, just waiting.

He could barely remember the impetus that had led him to join the NYPD. Probably reading too many Robert B. Parker novels. As he turned to the next page and began filling in the little boxes, he had to stop himself from reciting the old litany of his failures: Failure to recognize from the start that being a cop, let alone a homicide detective, was not for him. Failure to see that New York, which he'd loved the moment he'd arrived, had fallen from grace as he'd come to truly know the city. Failure to get the hell out at the first signs of disillusion.

He lifted his mug, but the coffee was gone. Seeking any escape he could from the forms on his desk, he headed to the coffeepot, past the rows of desks and all the chatter, past the men who loved the job, or at least tolerated the bullshit better. If Miguel had been here, at least he could have bitched to someone, but Miguel was a klutz and therefore out of commission basking in the attention of his wife and two kids.

Paula from vice was in the break room looking sharp as always. She was a tough kid, ambitious, and she'd never made any bones about the fact that she didn't give a damn about his predilection for books. Truthfully, he doubted she would have cared if his passion had been spiders or balloon animals. All Paula was interested in was a good time with no strings attached. Unfortunately, along with his deepening malaise about the job, he'd lost his old spark with women. Not that he didn't like them, he just wanted someone who could talk to him after. And not, for God's sake, about the job.

As for meeting other women, civilians, he always meant to get on top of that. Go to some lectures or book signings. But he never knew when he was going to get a call, and when he did finally make it home, he'd bury himself in a book, or, as was happening a lot lately, sleep.

"Bax, baby. How's it hangin'?"

"It's hangin' just fine."

She poured herself a cup of joe, then put the pot back on the burner. "I heard about what happened to Miguel. Bad luck."

"Clumsiness," he said, getting the pot back out to pour himself a cup.

"So, who you gonna partner with?" She leaned against one of the lockers, making sure her impressive breasts were given their due.

"Don't know. Don't care."

"That's right. You're leaving soon. Shame."

"Why a shame?"

Her red lips curled in a smile that had the subtlety of a wrecking ball. "Ah, come on, Bax. You know I've always thought you were a hell of a cop."

"Of course you have," he said, not believing her for a second. Not that he wasn't a good cop—he'd never compromised on the job no matter what. He wouldn't start now, either. He might be leaving the force, but he'd go out with pride.

"Not to mention you've got the best damn ass in the precinct."

He sipped the coffee, surprised that it tasted pretty good. "My ass and I thank you for the kind words. But now we have to go back to our desk and get to work."

She sighed dramatically. "It just breaks my poor heart. Such a fine-looking man. Such a waste."

"You could have any man you wanted, and you know it."

"Not any man." The lips turned to a pout. "Not you."

"You're not missing a thing," he said, meaning it. "Not a thing."

IT WAS JUST PAST TWO in the morning and Danny Austen was a no-show.

Jenna, Carlane and Mia had been hiding in the far corner at the big black circular bar at Erotique for over an hour sipping watermelon martinis and checking the door every five seconds. Before Erotique, they'd had a long, lingering dinner at Amuse Bouche, then they'd gone outside and hung out by the movie trailers. No luck finding Danny Austen anywhere.

"Can't you find out what he's doing?" Carlane asked. "Call room service. Maybe he's upstairs."

"We didn't see him go by and that's hard to miss with all the uproar he causes. He's probably working," Mia said. "These movie people have such bizarre hours."

"I don't want to go home without meeting him." Jenna checked the door again. "I don't have another night off until next week."

"The movie's not leaving any time soon," Mia said. "We'll catch him later."

"You don't get it." Jenna, who was in her early forties and one of the best concierges in the business, gave her a look. "I need to meet him now so he has time to fall completely in love with me before the shoot is over. Jeez."

"Oh, that's right. Sorry." Mia grinned. "I have to say, he's so much better-looking in person. So tall. And he's got these really wide shoulders and those little tiny hips that are so incredible. It's been very difficult to maintain my professional demeanor."

"Your what with who?" Carlane finished off her drink with a flourish. "Honey, you drool just like the rest of us plebeians. We're groupies, plain and simple. How pathetic that we're so enamored of a freaking movie star. He's probably a pig and a lout, but do we care? No."

Mia frowned as she looked around the bar. She'd changed from her black tux and pink bow tie uniform into black jeans and a white peasant blouse. She'd even put on fresh makeup, and for what? If they did see Danny Austen she wasn't going to talk to him. The last thing she wanted was to appear unprofessional. All she cared about was giving her friends a little treat. "There's nothing wrong with having fantasies. In fact, it's good for the imagination. Besides, I've practically forgotten what it's like to be with a real man. I mean, who has time for dating?"

"Well, you never look," Jenna said. "Honey you've got to lighten up. The world won't come to an end if you think about something other than the job."

"Hey, that's not all I think about."

Jenna raised her eyebrow. "Your mystery novel obsession doesn't count. Nor do your puzzle collections, your trivia books, or the fact that you'd rather dig up bat hearts than go ogle Danny Austen."

"Oh, come on. I'm not that bad. Besides, I do think about men. I just haven't met one who's worth the trouble."

"Mia, sweetie." Carlane signaled the bartender. "The right guy isn't any trouble. Unfortunately, most of the men in this city are deviants or married or gay or all three."

Mia sighed and they all just sat there for a moment, wallowing in the sadness of their pitiful love lives. "Okay," she said, finally. "I'm going down to Exhibit A to see if they're shooting. If they are, I'll try and get you two in to meet him, okay?"

"Please," Jenna said. "Give me something delicious to dream about tonight."

Mia hopped down from the bar stool. "I'm on the case. You guys hold the fort, and if he walks in here while I'm gone, call me immediately."

Both women saluted, and Mia strode off toward the elevator.

Amuse Bouche, the restaurant that was connected to the hotel, had closed at midnight. At twenty-till, there'd still been a line. The big draw, aside from the incredible food, was the outdoor patio. It didn't hurt that the film trucks were still there, although most of them were parked on side streets or in the underground garage, or that there was an even chance of seeing really famous people walk by. Just ask the paparazzi. Talk about people who never slept. They covered the hotel front and back 24/7. She often wondered when and how they went to the bathroom. They sure as heck didn't use the hotel's facilities.

She got to the elevator and hit the down button, feeling her martini, but not too strongly. She probably wouldn't have another. Maybe some water, just so she wouldn't wake up with a headache.

She fished her lip gloss out of her pocketbook. After a hasty application, she put a mint in her mouth, got her small compact out to dust her nose, then checked her hair and eye makeup. Nothing was too dreadful, but she wasn't going to pose for *Vogue* anytime soon.

By the time she stepped out of the elevator, she was as good as she was gonna get.

The hall was suspiciously quiet all the way past the black Exhibit A logo and when she got to the nightclub's door, there was nothing to see but a big sign that said HOT SET. She assumed it was not okay to go inside and move stuff around. But if she didn't touch anything…

She hadn't been in Exhibit A since the movie company had rented it. They'd changed things, of course. They had to make the room fit their story, right?

She turned around and went back to the door to peek inside. It wasn't as dark as she'd assumed. Soft lights were lit all around the perimeter. The white tables that normally were in the center of the room had been pushed to the far left wall. The booths and sofas hadn't been disturbed, but the wall art, the chandeliers, most everything that would immediately identify the club as one of the most exotic and sensual in the city had been covered over or replaced by pretty mundane stuff.

She stepped inside, wondering why they'd chosen such a boxy bandstand with such awful orange curtains, but then she had no idea what the movie was about. Maybe she could score a script—that would be interesting and fun. She'd never read one before, although she was a certified movie addict.

She went over to the bar area, trying to figure out if the small glasses on the counter were drinks to be used in the next scene or just a mess left from the crew. Just as she was about to investigate up close, she tripped, fell forward, saving herself from a serious crash at the last second by catching the edge of the bar.

Shaken, worried she'd ruined some vital piece of movie set, she turned to see what she'd fallen over. Her breath left her in a strangled scream as she saw the body.

It was a guy, a big guy, and oh, God, there was blood, a lot of it, all over the shiny floor. Some seeping around long, thick cables. But her gaze went straight to the face, because he was on his back, he was staring up, and even in the shadows she could see he was dead. Really dead.

She moved toward him, careful not to step in the blood. The guy had on jeans and a plain shirt, and oh, crap, the blood didn't quite cover a gaping wound that stretched across his neck.

If she moved just a couple of inches to the right the light from behind her would illuminate his face. With a quick gulp of air she steeled herself then moved those few steps. The light fell right on the face. His face.

Gerry Geiger's face.

Her hand went to her mouth as she fought another scream. As the blood rushed from her head. As the urge to run propelled her toward the door. But then she remembered her job. The hotel. Her responsibility.

With shaking hands, she pulled her personal cell from her purse and dialed 9-1-1. She could be sick later.

2

BAX HATED CELEBRITIES. He hated the paparazzi. He hated movie people in general.

Who was he kidding, he hated pretty much everyone and everything in this town, particularly in this precinct.

His pain was somewhat mitigated by the fact that he'd pulled Grunwald as his partner on this. He was a good detective, hungry, and a fiend for detail. Which meant that Grunwald would be doing the paperwork on this baby, while Bax would focus on the footwork. If only Grunwald's breath didn't always smell like an especially foul combination of stale cigarettes and some acid reflux.

They had already been briefed by the first officer on scene, and now it was time for Bax to interview the first witness on scene. He glanced over to where she stood in the corner near all the cameras, lights, director's chairs and cable. Her name was Mia Traverse and she worked at the hotel. It didn't surprise him that she was pretty. One of those tiny girls, barely five feet, who looked as if a strong wind could carry them across the street. She hugged herself as she snuck glances at the body.

Bax was anxious to talk to her before the swarm that always surrounded murder descended. As he got closer he saw she wasn't exactly as delicate as he'd first imagined.

She looked upset all right, but her back was straight, her eyes serious and focused. He nodded. "Detective Milligan. You found the body?"

She nodded back. "I came down to see if they were still filming. I hadn't been to the club since they'd rented it."

"You always here at two in the morning?"

"I'm a concierge for Hush. My shift ended at five, but I had dinner and drinks here with some friends. They were hoping to meet Danny Austen."

"And?"

"There's not much else to say. The club was empty. I was trying to be careful, not to touch anything. I tripped over—"

Her voice had cracked. So she wasn't quite as in control as she'd like.

A big light came on behind him, and he wondered if they'd used one that was already here, or if the newly arrived CSI guys had brought their own. He kept his eyes on the woman.

Flipping a page in his notebook, he moved a little closer to her. "You're Mia Traverse?"

"That's right."

"Concierge. And you got here…?"

"You mean, to Exhibit A?"

"Yes."

"Ten after two. I remember looking at my watch as I got out of the elevator."

"You came down here by yourself."

She nodded.

"Did you know the deceased?"

"Only to chase him out of the hotel. He was here all the time, always trying to sneak in. Everyone was always on Geiger alert."

"What do you mean, everyone?"

"All the staff of course, but the movie people, too. No one could stand him. He had no boundaries."

"What boundary did he cross tonight?"

"He tried to get into the restaurant earlier today. Uh, yesterday. I saw the security guys kick him out. But that was nothing unusual. We've found him in guest rooms, in the supply closet. One day he wore a disguise and tried to blend in with the movie crew but they caught him right away."

"So nothing unusual. No fights, no threats."

"I wouldn't swear to no threats. But I personally didn't see anything you would call unusual."

Bax jotted down a few things, then looked up. Her face had changed, brightened.

He said nothing. Just waited.

She cleared her throat, her eyes shifted to the right. "I think that's everything."

"Do you?"

"I—"

She was interrupted by the "Ride of the Valkyries." It wasn't a full orchestra and it was tinny as hell, but there was no mistaking the music. Mia turned sharply and grabbed her purse from the bar top behind her and a few seconds later the music stopped as she answered her phone.

He fought a smile at her choice of ring tones. His phone rang. Just rang. But this slip of a girl, uh, woman had picked Wagner. As she told her caller that she couldn't talk and would explain things later, he perused his notes. She didn't seem to know much about what had happened, at least not about the murder, but she knew something. He'd have to watch her, find a way to get her to talk.

He knew a couple of concierges and they were notoriously close-mouthed. He had no doubt Mia Traverse was the same. But he also knew that the concierge of a hotel could be a font of information. A central clearing house for juicy tidbits about the staff and the guests.

He'd find out what she knew. She might believe that discretion was the better part of valor, but there was no valor in a slit throat.

"Is that all, Detective?"

He looked at her once more. At her wispy haircut with the short bangs, at the artfully applied makeup that highlighted her big eyes. He wondered briefly if they'd hired her just for her looks, then dismissed the thought. This was one hell of a famous hotel, owned by the one celebrity heiress who seemed to have gotten her act together, but still, Hush was known as the sex hotel. Someone had told him each room came equipped with sex toys. Not only that, but video cameras. "Interesting."

"What's that?" she asked.

"Nothing. Just…"

The way she looked at him, her big eyes wide, her lips slightly parted… Her skin looked soft and sweet and he wondered how old she was. For her job at this kind of hotel he'd have guessed she would have to be around his age, but she didn't have that jaded New Yorker look.

"Detective?"

"You just focus on taking care of the paying guests," he said, his tone gruffer than he'd intended. "We've got this covered, you understand?"

The surprise on her face wasn't nearly as revealing as the pink blush that covered her cheeks. He'd hit the nail on the head. She could be useful, if he played her just the right way. This was going to be a high-profile case, hitting the papers with a roar. He was the lead on this, and it was going to be one of his last. No way he was leaving without solving this one. Whatever it took.

MIA PICKED HER WAY OUT of Exhibit A, careful not to disturb anything. She even managed not to look at Geiger's body. At the thought she shivered again, something that had been happening a lot. It surprised her that she'd been clearheaded at all as she talked to that detective.

Two things niggled at her as she headed for the employee lounge and her locker. The first was that last thing the detective had said. As if he'd known somehow that she planned on doing a bit of investigating on her own. After all, this was her hotel, and if she could use her sources to get to the bottom of things, all the better. But still, how had he...?

She nodded at a couple of graveyard-shift folks sitting at the tables in the cafeteria, sipping coffee. Casual, as if a murder on the premises didn't faze them. Or maybe they didn't know yet. She expected that to change within the hour. One thing about Hush—gossip was a constant, mostly to do with the employees themselves, but sometimes about the guests. She had every reason to believe that the murder would stir up all kinds of information and she intended to be smack dab in the middle of that.

She pushed through the door that led to the lockers and as she reached for her lock, she remembered the other niggle. Detective Milligan was way the heck too hot.

He probably wouldn't appeal to Carlane or Jenna. They favored the pretty ones, like Danny Austen. Not her. She liked her men rugged. Lived in. A strategic scar never hurt anything, either.

She'd always been that way. She'd preferred Bogie to Cary Grant in the old films, and even today her celebrity tastes slid more toward Clive Owen than Brad Pitt.

She gathered her things together slowly as she recalled the detective's dark eyes and that strong jaw. His hair was short, but not fatally so, and messy in a good way. He must have been a foot taller than her, and wow, his hands had been really large. Wouldn't they feel just incredible on her back? Or lower?

She turned to make sure she was alone, suddenly embarrassed by her own thoughts. Not that she didn't have erotic thoughts. She did. As many as any other healthy woman. Nothing wrong with that at all, unless maybe you had them five seconds after finding a dead body.

Okay, so not five seconds, but close enough. Sheesh.

She'd never seen a dead body before. Even though she watched all those shows that pride themselves on how gross they can get, she still hadn't been prepared for the real deal.

Gerry Geiger had crossed someone's line. Crossed it big-time. So he'd been killed. And his ever-present camera snatched.

So what had he captured that had been worth his death? That was the big question. The major puzzle.

She slammed her locker shut and walked toward the back entrance. No public transportation for her tonight. She was taking a cab all the way to Brooklyn Heights, cost be damned.

Even at this ungodly hour the paps were in force. Naturally they'd seen the police vehicles and they were chomping at the bit to find out what had happened. She was escorted past them by one of the extra security guys and put into a taxi. Once she settled in for the ride, she thought again about what Geiger could have seen. It would have to be something really terrible. It wasn't that long ago that her first thought would have been adultery. But nowadays, who cared enough about that to kill? According to the tabloids, people, especially show biz people, cheated every day. Revolving beds were the norm. So, no, she didn't think it was about cheating.

Her best guess was that it somehow involved money. Lots and lots of money. That was what those people seemed to love most. That's what they protected at all costs. But what kind of photo could cost someone millions?

She'd have to think about that. But not until tomorrow. She didn't feel tired, but she knew that was just adrenaline, and by the time she got home, that would have dissipated and she'd crash. Which was good. The last thing she needed was to remember any details. Unless those details were all about one particular detective.

Her head fell on the seat back. Nope, even the delectable detective wasn't going to keep her awake tonight. Today. Whatever.

"Geiger was a bastard. There wasn't a person on the set who didn't want him dead."

Bax leaned back in the leather executive chair as he listened to yet another crock of bullshit from yet another movie big shot.

Piper Devon, the owner of the hotel, had given him an office in the lower level so he could conduct his interviews in relative peace. So far he'd spoken to the cinematographer, the script supervisor and two actors, both of whom thought Geiger's murder would somehow benefit their careers. None of them had given him anything useful.

He'd tried to get to the producer, but Oscar Weinberg had flown to Los Angeles early this morning. Of course he'd checked, and the travel plans had been made earlier in the week, but he still had Weinberg on his list. According to the associate producer, he would be back in three days. For now, Bax settled for talking to the director.

Peter Eccles was in his forties and his Hollywood life was written all over his face. Lines, wrinkles, fake perfect teeth, hair plugs and a completely immobile forehead made him appear more puppet than man. He was angry and nervous but his face looked weathered yet serene. Weird.

"Look, I had nothing to do with his death. I don't know who killed him and I've got to completely rearrange my shooting schedule because your people won't let us have the nightclub, so if you're done—"

"I'll let you know when I'm done," Bax said. "When's the last time you saw Gerry Geiger?"

"Yesterday. He was standing outside the hotel all afternoon."

"Did you speak with him?"

"No."

"When's the last time you spoke to him?"

Eccles raised a hand to his head, but stopped just before running it through his hair. "I don't know. I don't recall. We never actually spoke. It was more me yelling at him to get the hell away from my actors. Not what you'd call real dialogue."

"And you have no idea who would want to slit his throat?"

"I told you. Everyone. All of them. Probably hundreds of people I don't even know. He was a prick. A vampire. A waste of space."

"Did he ever take pictures of you?"

"I'm sure he did."

"Were any of them compromising?"

"You mean with my pants down? No. He never got that close."

Bax made a point of writing in his notebook, but it was mostly a list of what he needed to pick up at the store on his way home.

Across from him, Eccles tapped his leg with his fingers, his unease and impatience telegraphed from his very pores. "Are we done?" he asked again.

Bax wrote down cereal and cream, then checked the list to make sure he hadn't forgotten anything. When he was satisfied he looked into Peter Eccles's dark, furious eyes. "For now."

Eccles shot up and marched out of the office, slamming the door behind him.

Bax thought about smiling, but it wasn't worth it. Eccles was a jerk. They were all jerks. He doubted he'd get anything useful from even one of the players. He'd have to do some serious digging. Talk to Geiger's paparazzi buddies. He'd put the wheels in motion to get a background check on all these movie people and on Gerry and Sheila Geiger. Grunwald was going to have his hands full.

And then he'd talk to Mia Traverse. He still wasn't sure about his approach yet, but one thing was in her favor. She was young, eager. It was a pretty safe bet she was already digging around the hotel, trying to find out all she could about Geiger and the movie crew. Bax wanted to know it all. Every detail. But he didn't want to come right out and ask her to be his informant. He knew her first priority was the hotel and her job, which didn't negate the fact that she was plugged into the world of Hush. No, this was going to be about finesse, not force.

He went back to his original notes. It bothered him that the camera hadn't been found. It bothered him that Geiger was a sleaze, that everyone despised him, that most of the people staying in the hotel were suspects. At the moment the only people he could unequivocally eliminate as suspects were Piper Devon and Mia Traverse. Devon been at a very public function last night, her alibi confirmed by photographs in the *New York Post*. Traverse had been with her girlfriends in and around the hotel.

He wondered what she might have seen. Who. She may well know the killer's identity without even realizing it.

That was one interview he wasn't dreading in the least.

"SLIT. FROM EAR TO EAR. It was beyond horrible." Mia looked around the cafeteria, sure everyone was staring at her, wondering. Not if she'd killed Geiger, but if she knew something more than she'd told the police.

The truth was, she didn't. Not yet. But she didn't do a thing to dissuade people from the idea that she did. Know stuff. Any stuff.

Her lunch companion, Theresa, the head of housekeeping, had been a buddy for a long while and they often ate together, so that wasn't going to raise any eyebrows. What most of the staff didn't think about was Theresa's unbelievable information-gathering resources.

The maids.

It was the same in all hotels in Mia's experience. Guests, especially the upper echelon, didn't see the maids. They didn't speak to them, they didn't interact with them. Therefore, maids were not real. They were robots that cleaned and vacuumed. Mia had always felt badly that so few patrons tipped the maids, considering the crap the poor things had to put up with.

In this instance, it wasn't the crap they had to clean that had her hunkering down with Theresa, it was the stuff they saw.

"I saw dead bodies two times," Theresa said.

She was eating an empanada that smelled so good Mia was cursing her yogurt. But then Theresa was five-ten at least, statuesque and curvy. Not her five-two with barely a curve to be seen.

"One was just an old guy who had a heart attack. That was okay, but the second one, oh, baby."

"What?"

Theresa leaned closer. "Autoerotic asphyxiation."

"No."

"Yes. And you know what was the worst part?"

"What?"

"He was alone. I found him on the bathroom floor, his hand still on his wing wang. He'd strangled himself with his own belt, and let me tell you, it took some doing. He was blue. His tongue stuck out." She shivered, making her long, dark hair shimmer. "It put me off my soup, you know what I mean?"

Mia nodded as she took another spoon of key lime yogurt. "I do."

"I'm not surprised," Theresa said, just before taking another bite. Releasing another dose of that delectable scent into the air. Cumin. Cilantro.

Swallowing her urge to grab the empanada out of her friend's hand, Mia focused. "Not surprised about Geiger?"

"That's right, chica. I knew that man was going to get himself into hot water."

"Why, what do you know?"

"He was inside the director's suite the night he was killed."

"Eccles's suite?"

Theresa nodded.

Mia was almost going to ask her if she was sure, but of course she was. "How did you find out?"

"Room service. Andy served them late last night. He saw Geiger in the mirror. This morning Yolanda found a piece from his camera. It was in a bag with his initials on it. They'd done some serious drinking. Most of the bottle of scotch was gone."

"Whoa. What did she do with the camera thingy?"

"Nothing. Yolanda knows better than to take something from a guest's room."

Mia sat back, stunned. Peter Eccles was a really famous director, although she'd heard somewhere that he'd lost his deal with Paramount, which had cost him a pretty penny. This shoot was supposed to give him that boost he needed to get back on the A list.

She wondered what Eccles had to hide. Had Gerry caught him stealing from the film budget? Sleeping with someone he shouldn't? She seemed to remember something about Eccles in the tabloids, but it had been too long ago and she hadn't paid much attention. She wasn't exactly a tabloid kind of gal.

But she knew someone who was. Dear sweet Carlane. She read the tabloids—all of them, not just Page Six— every single day. Bless her little heart.

"Mia?"

Theresa was looking at her with one of her patented

eyebrow raises. That alone kept her housekeeping staff on the ball.

"Sorry. I was just thinking."

"Don't think too hard, chica. Just because two men had a drink together doesn't make one of them a killer."

"I know. But still, it's curious, isn't it?"

"Yes, it is. In fact…" She looked around to make sure no one was eavesdropping. "Meet me in an hour in housekeeping. I'm going to talk to the girls who work the suites. And I'm going to see if I can get that camera bag."

"Deal. But don't do anything foolish, okay?"

"Yolanda told me the bag was half hidden under the couch. If it's still there, I'm going to grab it. Oh, and Mia?"

"Yes?"

"Don't get yourself too worked up. I know how you love your mysteries and puzzles but this was *asesinato*, not a game.

Mia nodded, but she was already thinking about that camera bag, and what Gerry Geiger would be doing with Peter Eccles.

3

IT WAS ALMOST FIVE in the afternoon and Bax had had it with actors. There wasn't a single one who hadn't tried to manipulate the hell out of him, and he hadn't even gotten to the big stars.

The worst had been a woman named Nan Collins who acted like an A-lister when, according to the assistant director, she was no more than a glorified extra. She'd said she was insulted that she was being questioned, but it was pathetically clear that the idea of being associated with the real players was her dream come true. She hadn't given him anything but a headache. Finally, though, he could take a break. There were still so many people to talk to, particularly those with the most to lose, like Weinberg and the two big stars. The thought made his head throb.

He left his temporary office and took his time as he made his way to the lobby, debating whether to go home and get some sleep or continue the interviews. He let his gaze wander as he stepped off the elevator. The hotel's décor was art deco, the pictures were all nudes of the period and the air felt rarified, as if a bad smell wouldn't dare.

There were people here, most of them on the young side, the men in expensive suits, the women dressed in designer clothes with impossible heels.

He looked down at his brown jacket, his brown pants, his brown shoes. The only thing not brown about him was his shirt, which was beige. He hadn't been home to change since yesterday and it showed.

Screw it. It had been one hell of a frustrating day, full of sound and fury, signifying squat. There were so many fingerprints on the scene as to render them useless. Motives had clearly been on sale for a nickel, because everyone he talked to seemed to have more than one. At least he'd managed to keep the basement nightclub a crime scene despite some extraordinary pressure from the producer.

Bax thought about his interview with Geiger's wife. He'd seen her at five this morning and it had been a real slice. Sheila Geiger had fallen apart when she heard about her husband's death. The two of them had been married eight years, and according to her, he was a model husband. Sure, he spent about twelve hours a day chasing down any scandal he could find, but she was adamant that he was a good man, and that the stars were all backstabbing liars who needed him more than he needed them.

She wanted action. She wanted arrests. She wanted his camera back.

"Detective Milligan?"

Bax jumped at the voice behind him. Her voice. Mia Traverse's voice.

He turned to find her in her uniform, a black tuxedo jacket and skirt, white blouse, pink silk tie, and yep, she was just as pretty as he remembered. She came over, reminding him again how small she was. And that she smelled damn good.

"Is there something I can help you with?" she asked.

"Maybe. I understand the rooms all come with a video recorder."

She nodded. "Walk with me?"

He did as she headed for the reception area where the concierge services were conducted behind a curved, black lacquered desk. He waited as she went to her station. She checked to make sure there had been no calls, then put on one of those Bluetooth ear deals which always made him think of Uhuru from *Star Trek*.

"Each room has a small video recorder," she said, her attention squarely on him, "and each guest is given several blank tape cartridges. It's all part of the Hush amenities package."

"It's actually the tapes I'm interested in."

Her eyebrows rose. "Those are of a private nature. Meant for couples."

"I figured. On the other hand, someone might have taped something of a murderous nature."

She nodded solemnly. "Yes, it's possible. But I'm not sure how you'd ever find out."

"I was thinking that maybe together we could come up with a solution to that little problem."

"I'd love to help in any way I can, Detective, but those tapes are private. They become the property of the guest the moment they check in."

"What would a maid do if she found a tape that was open in a room where the guests have checked out?"

"Turn it in to lost and found."

"Okay. Would you check that out please? If there were any tapes left, I'll need to see them."

"I'll be happy to, but wouldn't the killer, if he taped

himself murdering Geiger, have made a point to take the evidence with him?"

"I doubt very much the killer would have filmed that session. That's not what I'm after. I think it's possible that one of the guests might have taped something that could give us a direction."

"Oh, I see."

He knew it was a long shot, but he had to try. "What about security cameras?"

"We do have cameras, althoug not in Exhibit A, or even that hallway."

"Where are they?"

"I can put you in touch with security. They know a lot more about it than I—" A chirping sound had come from a cell phone on her desk. She flipped it open and brought it to her ear.

"Concierge, Mia speaking. How may I help you?"

Bax watched and listened as Mia talked to her guest. She was calm, pleasant, and as she talked, she also typed, looking something up on the computer. The conversation was evidently about a pharmacy that delivered.

He checked out her work space, which was as tidy as she was. A large Rolodex, telephone books, three-ring binders. Just what he'd expect to see. He paused, however, when he saw what looked like a camera case. Taking a couple of steps to his right to get a better look, he was surprised to see the initials GG in gold script on the top.

When he looked back at Mia, it was clear from her blush she knew what he'd found. Bax sighed. He'd been right about her. Eager, enthusiastic. Nosy. A perfect informant. Ideal. Only, as an informant, he had to be damn careful with her. Not just so he wouldn't scare her off, either. He had to make sure that she remained a credible witness. Which meant she was completely hands-off. Which should have been no issue at all.

She finished with her phone call. "I was going to tell you about that."

"When?"

"Don't be mad. There's a story with it and—" The phone chirped again. She flicked her earpiece this time instead of picking up the cell and immediately put the caller on hold. "Tell you what," she said. "I get off work in fifteen minutes. It'll take me ten to change out of my uniform. Why don't you go to the bar and relax. I'll come get you and we can go to dinner. My treat."

"Twenty-five minutes?"

"And I'll be all yours."

He knew exactly what she meant but that didn't stop a momentary flash of a completely unprofessional nature.

She returned her attention to the guest as he walked toward the bar, wondering if his attraction to her was about hormones or homicide?

SHE HAD THE CAMERA CASE in her purse as they went to Maxwell's, a coffee shop she and most of the Hush crew frequented. It was no Amuse Bouche, but they had decent food and for Madison Avenue, they were reasonable.

Mia could tell he wanted answers, but he waited patiently as they were seated and placed their orders.

She brought out the bag as soon as the waitress left. "It's just a lens," she said. "No film, no camera."

"But it did belong to Geiger?"

"It did, yes. But that's not the interesting part."

The waitress came back with coffee for him, an iced tea

for her. When they were alone again, Mia leaned in. "It was found in Peter Eccles's suite and it was left there the night Geiger was killed."

The detective's expression changed. It wasn't dramatic. In fact, if she hadn't been watching closely, she'd have missed it. His eyes, a deep dark brown, widened a hair and his nice broad shoulders straightened.

He really was an attractive man. Even in his dull suit there was something about him that appealed to her. Not just his rugged good looks, either. Obviously, she barely knew the man but still she saw an intelligence about him. He might come off all stoic and unflappable, but there was a brain in there. How she knew, she wasn't sure, but she knew. She'd known from the first.

Over the years her ability to quickly gauge strangers had been developed and nurtured. Part of being a good concierge was to make and trust first impressions.

Even in the stressful situation of finding a body her radar had been active. Other parts of her had been active, too, which surprised her more.

Honestly, his looks weren't all that remarkable. Not compared to the movie stars and models who frequented the hotel. But he was sexy in his rumpled suit and his mussed hair. She kept finding herself wanting to touch him.

"Okay," he said. "I'll pay for dinner if you don't make me beg."

She realized she'd been staring instead of talking. "The maid found it in Eccles's room. Along with the remains of his scotch, which room service had delivered the night before."

"How did you get it?"

"I told you. I know people."

"Right."

"Listen, Detective. I shouldn't have the lens. It was a questionable move meant to help. If it came to light how I got it, good people could get hurt. I won't let that happen."

"I could compel you to tell me—"

"You could," she said, stopping him, "but you'd be cutting off your nose to spite your face."

"You want to be the go-between, I get it. While that might seem appealing or even exciting, it can also mean you'll be caught in the middle. We're talking murder here, Ms. Traverse. Not a game of telephone."

She'd thought about this since the moment Theresa had told her about the lens. The last thing she wanted to do was to impede the investigation. Hush didn't need the kind of publicity it was getting and the longer the killer was on the loose, the more it damaged the reputation of the hotel. Mia's first responsibility, as long as she didn't actually break the law, was to protect her employer. Second was to protect the staff. She could do both while still helping the detective, but only if he agreed to her terms. "I understand what's at risk. We all want this murder solved."

"What if it turns out to be someone from the hotel. Someone not involved with the movie?"

She sat back in the booth. "You think I want a killer working at Hush?"

He didn't say anything, but his eyes told her he wasn't completely convinced.

"Look, we have a lot of our staff assigned directly to the VIP guests. They're all very discreet though. If you try to talk to them, you'll get a whole lot of nothing. They trust me. They'll open up to me."

"There's a big difference between being discreet and obstructing justice."

"It's up to you. Your way, there's a lot of disruptions and rancor. My way, you catch the killer and everybody wins."

He laughed. "Confident, are we?"

She sat up straighter and willed herself not to blush. "Yes, I am."

He drank some more coffee, looked at her as if he was trying to see inside her head, but finally he nodded. "We'll try it your way. But you don't tell anyone you're talking to me, got it? And you don't hold anything back, even if it's not good for the hotel."

She stuck out her hand. "To the best of my ability, you have my word."

He shook, although the doubt was still in his eyes.

She didn't really want him to think too much more about their agreement, though. Time to change tactics. "You haven't been home since last night."

"No, I haven't."

"How come?"

"Part of the job."

"It must be interesting. What you do."

The look on his face said it was anything but. "Yeah. It is."

She sipped her tea, debating for a moment letting it go, but the heck with that. "How long have you hated being a detective?"

Now that got a reaction. Alarm, then what, anger? No, not quite.

"I don't hate my job."

"Really," she said.

"Okay. It's lost some of its allure."

"How come?"

His lips pressed together as if to keep his words from slipping out. Mia just waited. Like a good cop, she'd learned a lot over the years about the value of silence.

"The politics," he said, finally.

She had the feeling he knew exactly what she'd done. That he was throwing her a bone. "What do you mean?"

"Too much paperwork, too much political correctness. It makes it hard to do the real work."

"I can see that. You must be under terrible scrutiny. Everyone out there with cameras on their cell phones. Everyone ready to sue at the drop of a hat."

With her commiseration, his defensiveness seemed to mellow. "It was my own fault. I had a romanticized view of what I'd be facing. I was naive to think things would get better when I became a detective."

"But you solve crimes. You put bad guys away."

"Not as often as I should."

"Somehow I doubt it's your work that's at fault."

"Why would you think that?"

"I watched you last night. You were thorough, commanding. You didn't let anything slide. And here you are. Still at it even though you must be exhausted. Am I right?"

"You make it sound noble. It's not."

"That's a matter of opinion. I'm sure it's discouraging to jump though all those hoops but I don't think you hate the heart of the job. It takes a unique individual to face the worst of people day after day, and still want to do the right thing."

Bax shook his head, almost but not quite dismissing what she'd said. "How did you end up at Hush?"

"Changing the subject, are we?"

"Turnabout's fair play."

She grinned. "I wanted the job very badly. Hush is a unique hotel, with unique demands. I was lucky to be chosen."

"Okay, I have to ask," he said. "What's the business about the sex?"

She grinned shyly. "Hush is simply an adult hotel that caters to consenting, discriminating couples."

"Yeah, I saw that in the brochure. But I still don't get it."

"It's about pleasure, Detective. Unapologetic and so-phisticated. Visual, tactile, in fact all the senses are catered to. There's something for everyone from the massages at the spa to the unbelievable room service—"

"Yeah, about that. I've heard that a guest can order more than dinner."

"They can have massage or beauty services. Even their pets can have room service."

He wondered if she was being coy or naive. It was hard to tell with her. Damn, though, he wished she hadn't changed from the black tux. Not that she didn't look good in her red T-shirt and jeans, but the T was snug and Maxwell's was chilly.

Of course he was a moron for bringing up this topic. Just hearing her talk about catering to all the senses had made him uncomfortable. Bringing it back to business would help. "Those massage services wouldn't include special bonuses, would they?"

"Oh, you're talking about prostitution. No, that's not at all what Hush is about. Did you know that each room comes with an armoire stocked with sex toys?"

Okay, so Mia wasn't quite as innocent as her image would suggest. Shit. An armoire stocked with sex toys? He'd like to see those. See her. Touch— Damn it. "How does that work?" he asked, hoping she hadn't noticed his voice crack.

She unsuccessfully hid a snicker. "That would depend on the guest."

She was killing him here. On purpose. Because she could. Because she knew he was getting hard at her matter-of-fact voice, at that wicked smile. He cleared his throat. "No, I mean those kinds of amenities really couldn't be reused, could they?"

"It depends. Anything that has the possibility of contact with bodily fluids is replaced for each guest. But some of the toys are cleaned and reused. It's a very strict process with no room for error. You should come down sometime and see the operation. You'd be impressed."

"I'm sure I would," he said, desperate to change the subject. Thankfully, dinner arrived and Bax threw himself into eating his pastrami on rye. It wasn't quite as effective as a cold shower, but as long as Mia didn't talk about sex toys any more, he should be okay.

"A lot of people come to Hush expecting something lurid or tacky, but no one has ever left with that impression. It's hard, though, because the press is so myopic. Sex sells. The sleazier the better. And when you combine that with Piper Devon's reputation, which, I must say is totally distorted, then you get tabloid accounts full of insinuation and exaggeration. It's a shame."

Think of the sandwich. Not the sex. "But you keep getting the clientele you're really after."

"Mostly due to Piper and word of mouth."

"It doesn't hurt that the place is incredibly expensive."

"Our guests are of the belief that you get what you pay for. The higher the price, the more valued the service."

"Damn, you're good at this stuff."

"What stuff?"

He ignored the question as he finished the first half of his sandwich. He was finally settling down, getting some control. But he had to steer the conversation away from the goddamn sex. "Let me ask you something. You've clearly had to deal with the paparazzi since you started working there. Do you make deals with them? Give them exclusives in return for favors?"

"Sometimes. Always to the benefit of the hotel, though, and there are lots of paps who aren't ever considered for special favors."

"Like Gerry Geiger?"

She shook her head. "Geiger wasn't always this bad. We used to use him on occasion, but only because he played by the rules."

"Why do you think he changed?"

"I don't know. I figured it was about money. It always seems to be about that, though."

Bax made a mental note to dig deeper into Geiger's financial situation, although he knew Grunwald was already on top of it. What Bax wondered was if there were some hidden accounts, maybe under Sheila's name.

"Let me talk to Kit, our public relations manager," Mia said. "She'll let me know what the situation was with Geiger."

Bax nodded. Relaxed. Finally, he felt steady again, at least for the time being. "You went to school to become a concierge?"

"I studied hotel management. But I've been around hotels my whole life. Both my parents are concierges. That's what gave me the edge with Hush."

"Doesn't it bother you to have to coddle a bunch of overprivileged snobs?"

"I don't coddle. I perform a service. I do my best to see that the guests of the hotel have an exceptional experience."

"But aren't most of the requests things your guests could do for themselves if they'd only lift a finger or two?"

"Sometimes. But honestly, I don't see it that way. A lot of them are simply too busy to start checking the phone book or to find out where the closest luggage shop is. I know the city. I can make their stay more pleasant, easier. I have extraordinary connections, so I'm able to help the guests get the things they really need."

"I'm leaving," he said, apropos of nothing.

She put her fork down. "Now?"

He shook his head, surprised that he'd brought this up. He hadn't planned on telling her anything about himself. "In three months. I'm leaving the force."

She didn't seem too shocked, which made sense considering their earlier conversation. "Where are you going?"

"Boulder. I'm going back to school."

"That's wonderful. Studying law, or—"

"Literature."

Mia sat back in the booth. Now she seemed shocked. "Literature. Wow."

Oddly, he felt proud and embarrassed both when he should have felt neither. "I want to write. To teach."

"I'd very much like to hear that story," she said.

He tried to hold back a yawn and failed. "Maybe another time." When he looked at her again it was with a sleepy smile. "I have the feeling you're a very good concierge."

"That I am," she said.

He sat back in the booth as she took her tiny bites of blintzes, thinking that he should leave her to finish dinner alone. He needed to go home and get some sleep. Not that he hadn't done this a hundred times over the last ten years. Stayed up for twenty-four, thirty-six or more hours. It was part of the gig. What made him wonder about his mental state wasn't that he was sleepy. It was that all he wanted to do was sit in Maxwell's diner across from Mia Traverse and watch her eat. Sip her iced tea.

Nope, it didn't make a damn bit of sense. But there it was.

4

"I PREFER JANE AUSTEN, personally," Mia said as they returned to Hush later that night. *"Pride and Prejudice. Emma."* She gave herself a little hug. "So wonderful."

"Would my manliness come into question if I admitted I like her books, too?"

Mia looked up at him with a broad smile. "I think you're safe in that respect, Detective."

He slowed his pace, wondering if he was about to make a big mistake. Screw it. He only had three more months to get through, and they were going to be working together. "It's Bax."

The back of her hand brushed the back of his. The briefest of touches, probably an accident. And yet it made him feel things he hadn't felt in a hell of a long time.

"I know," she said. "Baxter Milligan. What I can't figure out is if the name is Irish or Scottish."

"Both is my guess. The Milligans were on the border between England and Scotland, from Wigtown, in fact. From what little my grandfather told me, the young lads had issues with geography."

"Have you been there?"

He shook his head. "But if the writing works out, I mean really works out, I might like to settle in Ireland."

"Won't you miss living here?"

"I don't think so," he said, his pace so slow they were almost standing still. Thing is, he didn't want the conversation to be over. "I don't have real close ties. A brother in California, a sister in Boston. We hardly see each other."

"Why not?"

He had to think a minute but before he could even suppose at an answer they were in front of the hotel.

Suddenly there was a crowd of people surrounding Mia. Someone shouldered him back a step, then a camera hit him in the ribs.

"Who killed Gerry Geiger?"

"Why are Bobbi and Danny only taking half their regular salaries?"

A dozen more questions shot like gunfire over the flashing camera lights. He ignored it all in his need to get to Mia, to get her out of the center of the storm. Taking no precautions, he barreled through, not caring one damn that there were cries of protest and pain. Especially when, to his horror, Mia yelped as she fell over some moron's camera case.

Bax was there in a heartbeat, kneeling down, scared shitless and mad enough to put the whole lot of them behind bars or worse.

"Mia?"

She blinked up at him. "Whoa. That wasn't very pleasant."

"No, it wasn't." He took her arm and helped her sit up as flashes went off all around them. He wanted to shove the cameras down some throats. For Christ's sake, they weren't celebrities. None of those pictures would mean a damn thing.

The moment he could see she hadn't been seriously hurt, he turned on the paparazzi. "Get the hell away from her."

Instant quiet. No more camera flashes.

"You found the body. Any clues there who killed Geiger?" some guy shouted from the edge of the crowd.

"Are Danny and Bobbi having an affair?"

"Why was Geiger on Weinberg's payroll since the Mexico shoot?"

"Come on, you must know something, huh!"

Bax checked Mia once more. "You okay? Should I get an ambulance?"

"No, no. I'm fine. Just a little bump on my butt is all."

"You sure?"

She squeezed his arm with her small hand. "Positive."

"Good," he said, then stood up, pulling her along with him. She seemed steady on her feet.

He swung around, lifting his badge as he faced the bulk of the crowd. "Two seconds and I'm taking you all in for a hard forty-two. Is that clear enough for you bastards, or do you want to get a tour of Rikers?"

The photographers flew apart as if blown by a tornado, and that's what Bax felt like. This whole event had been unacceptable and it was all he could do not to bust some heads.

Of course, most everything was unacceptable these days.

"I should have been more careful," Mia said as she brushed off the back of her jeans. "They never leave. I'm surprised they didn't catch us when we left for dinner."

"They were busy. Swarming in front of some other victims."

"I didn't notice."

"Are you really okay? I can get you to the hospital in a couple of minutes."

"I'm fine. But it's late. I should go, get home. So should you."

He took her elbow and led her into the hotel. It was calm and cool inside, with some good jazz coming from the bar. As they got closer to the reception desk, he saw that the restaurant was still busy, the bar packed. He wondered how many of the night crawlers were part of the film company. How many were there because they wanted to meet the celebrities.

"Thank you, Bax," Mia said as she stopped in front of the elevator. "I had a good time."

Her smile hit him again in that long-dormant center of his brain where women had once had free rein.

"You owe me the rest of your story."

"I haven't forgotten," he said.

She pressed the down button. "I've got to scoot to get my train. Be careful out there, Detective."

"I always am."

She left him standing in the lobby, under a picture of a very exotic naked lady who was sitting perilously close to a jaguar. He needed to go home. Get some sleep. Start tomorrow fresh and on his game. But hell, who was he kidding? There was no way he was letting Mia get home on her own.

MIA WENT TO THE LADIES room mirror to make sure she didn't have a big old bruise on her behind.

She wasn't about to freak in front of Bax, but wow, that had been really scary. For a minute there, she'd thought those whack jobs were going to trample her to death.

Bax. He'd asked her to call him by his first name. That meant something. And he'd been all over those paparazzi when she'd tripped. Just remembering his voice gave her the shivers. So forceful and commanding. She'd practically swooned into his arms, which, now that she thought about it, was pretty bizarre. She wasn't the swooning type. She was the one her friends called when swooning occurred.

So why was she feeling like such a *girl?*

And what had that one pap asked about Geiger and the Mexico shoot? Was she remembering right? Probably not. She'd been pretty distracted, what with falling on her behind.

Back in the locker room to fetch her backpack, she met up with Lorraine, one of Piper Devon's assistants. They talked a bit about the murder. Lorraine hadn't worked yesterday, but she'd heard all kinds of things today.

"Geiger's wife is planning to sue the hotel and the movie company for millions."

"Really?" Mia sat down on the bench, her backpack forgotten on her lap. "Did she call Piper?"

Lorraine sat down, too. She was about Mia's age, but they didn't know each other well. Lorraine was in grad school, so her schedule was hell, but she was nice. And observant.

"She called Piper all right. Of course, Piper knows how to handle this kind of thing. She invited the wife to lunch. Tomorrow."

"At Amuse?"

Lorraine nodded, then wiped a stray blond hair from her cheek. She, like many of the women here at Hush, tried to emulate Piper Devon's look. They all wanted to appear as sophisticated and as together as Piper. Only a few came close.

"Of course, Trace is going to be there, too. She'll just introduce him as her husband. Geiger's wife won't even know he's the hotel's attorney until it's too late."

"Odd though, don't you think, that Geiger isn't even buried yet and his wife is all about the lawsuit?"

"Look what her husband did for a living."

Mia nodded. "That's true. Greedy doesn't even begin to cover it."

Lorraine looked into the bathroom, making sure they weren't being overheard. "Did you know that Danny Austen had something going on with Geiger?"

"No he did not."

"I swear."

"Something sexual?" Mia asked, lowering her voice to a whisper.

"So I've been told."

"I thought he was trying to get tight with that actress. You know, the redhead?"

"Yeah, Nan. I met her. She seemed sweet and all, but she wasn't shy about Danny Austen. Paul saw her in Austen's trailer wearing his bathrobe."

"So if Danny is with Nan—"

Lorraine shrugged. "I don't know. I suppose if you're famous enough, you can have everybody. Maybe for them it doesn't matter what the sex is as long as it's sex."

"Still, Danny Austen with Geiger? I find that difficult to believe. Geiger was a parasite. Danny could get anyone he wanted."

"You're probably right. Although…"

"What?"

"Jeff Crown, the guy from accounting? He said there were some pretty suspicious charges coming from Danny's room."

"How would he know?"

"Yeah. You're right. I think everybody wants to be on the inside, you know? He's probably full of crap."

"Yeah. Probably."

"I gotta go," Lorraine said. She closed her locker. "See ya."

Mia hugged her backpack as she stared at her locker. That business about Danny Austen made no sense. But then, she didn't really know a lot of famous people. She wouldn't have believed Geiger having drinks with the director, and that turned out to be true.

Or was it?

No, it was true. Andy, Theresa's room-service source, wouldn't lie about that. Mia had no idea if Jeff Crown would. She'd best take it all with a big grain of salt. She'd keep her ear to the ground. That's all. She'd just listen.

A few minutes later, she was going out the back door to make a beeline to the subway, hoping to get past the paps without tripping or being trampled. Only she didn't have to worry because there was Bax, sitting on the pony wall in the garage, looking rumpled and tired and wonderful. Not a paparazzi in sight.

"What are you doing here?"

"Driving you home."

"You don't know where I live."

"Doesn't matter."

"I'm in Connecticut."

He looked a little startled, but then his unflappable face came back. "Then we'd better get going."

"I'm kidding," she said. "You don't have to take me home. The subway's right over there," she said, pointing to her right.

"My car's right over there," he said, pointing to his left.

"I live in Brooklyn Heights."

"Great," he said, standing with a distinctive knee pop. "It's right on my way."

She narrowed her eyes. "Why do I doubt that?"

"Because you're a suspicious woman. Come on. Let's do this."

She followed him to a somewhat new Ford Taurus that she would have immediately pegged as an unmarked police car. He held the door for her, and she wasn't surprised to find the inside was impeccably clean.

Watching him as he came around, she wondered if he was just being nice, or if he had more on his mind than simply seeing her home.

He didn't seem the kind of guy that would want more. Especially now that they'd established their working relationship. But then, maybe he didn't see a problem with that. If she were honest with herself, she'd admit the idea had its merits.

How long had it been since she'd been this interested in a guy? It felt like forever, but it was actually about eight months. Jean-Jacques had been nice enough. Certainly his European charm had seduced her and his accent had made her giddy. But in the end, they were both too caught up in their work worlds to have anything meaningful.

"Brooklyn Heights," Bax said as he settled in the car. He started it up and they drove slowly through the pack of photographers lying in wait. He said something low that she didn't quite catch.

"What was that?"

"A subliminal message."

She laughed. "You think it worked?"

"Nope. They're still there."

For a while, she just sat back and watched him drive. It was still rush hour, so traffic slogged. She didn't mind. She liked the way he maneuvered the car, not shy, but not in a death match, either. It would take them a while to get to the Brooklyn Bridge and across. For once, she was glad she didn't live closer to Midtown.

"Where do you live?" she asked, as they made the last turn before the bridge.

"Park Slope."

"Oh."

"I told you."

"I'm not right on your way."

"Close enough."

"You live alone?"

He looked at her as if the question surprised him. "Yeah."

"Not me. I have two roommates. Luckily, I don't see them too often. One has a boyfriend and the other works nights. It's not bad."

"Roommates. I don't think I could do that again."

"You had a bad experience?"

"I'm not easy to live with."

"Good to know."

He looked at her again.

She could hardly believe she'd said that out loud. My word, wasn't she the brave one. Which reminded her. "I heard something."

"When?"

"In the locker room."

"Okay. I assume it was about the murder."

She told him everything she could about her conversation with Lorraine. He seemed quite dubious about the Geiger-Danny Austen connection. Not at all about Geiger's wife.

"How reliable is this source of yours?"

"She's not one to make stuff up, but she did say it was all second hand info. I think the rumor mill at Hush is on over-drive, but you might want to check into those room charges."

He nodded as they inched their way across the bridge. "I'm not shocked about Sheila Geiger. I got the impression she wasn't all that upset that her husband was dead, although damn, she put on a good show."

"I wonder…"

"What?"

"What her rationalization is."

"For what?"

"Her life. Her husband. No one does something they know is wrong. People rationalize the most horrible things. The paparazzi, they all believe they're not doing anything wrong. They say the celebrities want their pictures taken. The public wants to buy those pictures. I guess I can't argue with that."

"Only?"

"It feels so wrong to me. I've seen them at their worst, like a pack of wolves. There's no mercy, no quarter given. Everyone and everything is fair game."

"What do you think is behind her suing the hotel?" he asked.

"She's thinking about her bank account. With hubby gone and unable to take those money-making pictures, a gal has to do what a gal has to do."

"And a job is out of the question."

"I think in her mind, yes," she said. "It is."

He sighed. "Boulder sounds better every day."

"I've never been to Colorado. I hear it's just gorgeous."

"Yep. Green everywhere you look. Great skiing. The English department is top notch. It's quiet. A man can think. See the stars."

"Big change."

"Welcome change."

"I would imagine so. All that death. All those rationalizations."

He reached over with his right hand and touched her left. He didn't hold it or squeeze it. He just touched her. Then he was gone.

"Where to?"

She realized they were approaching the Brooklyn side of the bridge. They hadn't talked all that much, but there had been pauses. Long ones. Now she was almost home.

"It's a right on Henry Street, a left on Remsen."

The traffic didn't ease up until they were almost at her building. Should she ask him up? Would he assume?

Of course there was no parking space for miles around her old brick building. There never was. It didn't seem to faze Bax. At her address he simply double parked, reached under the seat and got the bubble light that transformed the car from unmarked to quite distinct. And legal.

"I'll walk you up."

She didn't wait for him to open her door. There was a tiny thrill, however, in walking away from the car, Bax's hand on the small of her back. By the time they got inside, she was squarely fifty-fifty on the question of asking him to stay. Well, maybe sixty-forty.

They rode up to the fourth floor along with one of her many, many neighbors. Not one she knew by name. Just a woman who kept giving Bax sidelong glances.

Finally, they were at her front door. He didn't seem to be anxious to leave as she dug out her keys. Once the door was unlocked, she didn't know what to do.

He made it simple.

"What time do you get to the hotel in the morning?"

"A quarter to eight, if the trains are on time."

"I'll meet you at the subway," he said. "You lock up as soon as you're inside."

"Oh. Okay."

He bowed just a little, just with his head. When he looked at her again, Mia's throat tightened as she held her breath. His eyes had darkened and even though she could tell he had meant to walk away, he just looked at her.

It was as if the rest of the universe darkened and slipped away, leaving the two of them, straddling a line that probably shouldn't be crossed. Bax swallowed and her gaze moved to his Adam's apple, then back up to the stubble on his jaw, the slight parting of his lips. There was something unreal about him like this. A man that rugged shouldn't look so hungry. Or maybe it was the other way around.

He leaned closer to her. Not by much. Not enough.

Her own lips parted, willing him to cross the threshold and kiss her, darn it.

But he stopped. Suddenly. As if he'd been slapped into his role as cop, as protector. He swallowed once more as he stepped back. "Lock up now," he said, although with a much gruffer voice.

Mia watched him turn away, then she closed the door and locked it. But she didn't move for a long while.

What to make of Baxter Milligan? She hadn't a clue.

5

WHAT THE MOVIE PEOPLE called a trailer and he called a motor home was in the underground garage at Hush. It was a Winnebago-type deal times ten. Plush carpets, flat-panel TV, leather couches, marble counters. It was a hell of a lot nicer than Bax's apartment and it made him wonder yet again about the public's take on heroes. All Danny Austen did was dress up and pretend, and for that he got millions, adoration, trailers, women. It didn't help that Bax had a headache and that he'd had to come to Austen instead of Austen coming to him.

He leaned back in the incredibly comfortable captain's chair, waiting while Austen changed. Anxious to get the interview over with, Bax fiddled with his notebook, his pen, and kept thinking not about Danny Austen or Gerry Geiger but Mia Traverse.

As promised, he'd met her at the subway exit and made sure she got into the hotel safely. She'd had to go to her locker and change. He'd stood there like a damn fool long after the elevator had taken her away.

If she'd only known how virtuous he'd been last night. Okay, virtuous and tired. But man, he'd thought about her all the way home. And first thing this morning.

The universe had a wicked sense of humor.

He had to stop. This was the job. She was his informant. There was no way he could mix that with anything personal. Not just because it might taint her as a witness but because it would be completely inappropriate.

Not that such things hadn't happened. He knew one cop, a good detective by the name of Wilson, who'd been assigned to protect a witness. She'd been married at the time, and so had he, but three months after the trial they both filed for divorce. He'd gone to the wedding.

No one ever asked Wilson if they'd started screwing around while he was on the clock. No one had to ask. Wilson was still in the department, only now he was a desk jockey. Probably because his new wife didn't want him protecting anyone else.

It didn't matter that Bax was leaving. He wanted his career to end as it had begun. With self-respect. With a sense of pride. He just wished he didn't find her so damned attractive.

With a shake of his head he banished thoughts of Mia and focused once again on Danny Austen's world. On the table next to him there was a script for this movie, a couple of other scripts and a boatload of tabloid magazines, most of them with Austen on the cover.

Bax wondered if any of the cover shots had been taken by Gerry Geiger. Danny Austen was connected to Bobbi Tamony on two covers, but several other stars on other magazines. Was any of it true? Or were these just convenient lies to hide another side of the famous heart-throb? The last thing Bax wanted to do was give those rags a moment of attention, but they might play a key role in this investigation. That horrible fact made his head hurt worse.

"You want a drink?"

Bax looked up to find Danny standing in front of the refrigerator. Danny got himself one of those high-energy drinks with loads of sugar and caffeine.

"You have any coffee?"

Danny offered a smile so brilliant it made Bax wince. He had to give it to the guy—he looked every inch the movie star. He was tall and it appeared that he was religious about his workouts. Still, there was something slightly off about him. The hair, the eyes, the teeth, they were all perfect. Had the perfection come first, or was it a natural progression of becoming a star? Not that it mattered. Perfection at any time wasn't natural. People were flawed. If Austen's blemishes weren't on the outside, they were surely on the inside.

"Hold on." Danny picked up a walkie-talkie and pressed the button. "Riva?"

A voice came back, a woman, very clear. "I'm here."

"Can you bring me some coffee?" Danny turned to Bax. "Cream? Sugar?"

"Yes," he said.

"A whole service, 'kay?"

"Right there," she said.

Danny put the walkie-talkie down, then sat across from Bax in a matching chair. "So, hell of a thing, Gerry getting killed, huh?"

"Yeah," Bax said. "A hell of a thing."

Austen widened his eyes. "You have any suspects?"

"Lots. Let's try and make you not one of them, shall we?"

The guy winked at him. "I like your attitude. How can I help?"

Bax wondered whether the wink was a facial tic, or just

something movie stars thought made them seem more accessible. Personally, he preferred to think it was a tic. "Want to tell me what you were doing the night of the murder?"

"Nothing special. I was released at ten, then I went to my suite and took a shower."

"Released?"

"Yeah, I was finished shooting for the day. They try to release me before we go into overtime."

"You get overtime?"

"Sure. I'm SAG."

"Screen Actors Guild."

"And our hours are monitored. Not only do they have to watch our daily work times, but weekly as well. It's pretty expensive to go over with some of us. Well, me and Bobbi. The last thing Oscar wants is for us to go even a penny over budget."

"You've worked with him several times over the last six years, haven't you?"

Danny nodded. "He's done a lot for my career. I owe him. Which doesn't change the fact that he's notorious when it comes to the budget. Especially now."

"Why now?"

"Check the grosses over the last three years. *The Reformer? Black Sunset?* They both hemorrhaged money. He's got a lot riding on this picture."

"So after you showered…"

"I stayed—"

His recitation was interrupted by a knock on the trailer door. A second later, a young woman entered, carrying a tray with a carafe of coffee and all the accoutrements, including some donuts and muffins.

She was pretty, but then most of the people working on the movie were. Even those who would never be in front of the camera.

She set the tray on the table, then turned with a big smile to Austen. "Is there anything else I can do for you?"

He touched her in a way that made it perfectly clear her offer extended way beyond coffee. "No, thanks, Darlin'. We're all set."

With a coy glance and a slight blush, Riva left the building.

Bax wondered what it would be like to have any woman, any time. Exhausting would be his best guess. He poured himself a cup of coffee, the smell alone making his head feel better. Before he drank, however, he pulled Austen back on track. "You stayed...?"

"In. My room."

Bax settled back in his chair. "You stayed in your room all night?"

"All night."

"Alone?"

Austen laughed. "No, not alone. I was with Riva."

"The woman who was just here."

"Yep."

Bax sipped his coffee. He had no doubt Austen had been with Riva, but on that particular night? Something told him no. "Did you order room service?"

"As a matter of fact, we did."

"Great. What did you have?"

The actor smiled brightly again. "Nothing special. Dinner."

"What time?"

"I didn't look at the clock, Detective."

"But you didn't leave the room until morning."

"My call was at seven. But then we had the force, so—"

"Force?"

"Majeure. Because of the murder. We were shut down through no fault of the production company. They call it that, you know, for insurance purposes."

"I see. So you didn't know about Gerry Geiger's death until seven that morning."

"That's right."

"When was the last time you spoke to Geiger?"

Again, the smile. "That day. He tried to get some pictures. Just like he always did."

"What kind of pictures?"

"Nothing special. Coming out of the hotel. That kind of thing."

"You didn't know him, aside from him trying to take your picture?"

"That's right. He was just a pap. Just like all the others."

Bax put his cup down. He really wanted more coffee, but he needed to get to Riva before Austen had a chance to talk to her. "All right then. I think we're done. For now."

"Sure you don't want a donut?"

"I'm sure."

Austen leaned forward, placing his elbows on his knees. The smile came back, only this one wasn't meant to dazzle, at least not in the same way. "You know, I can help you with that headache."

"Pardon me?"

"Your headache. I studied some massage back in the day. Honest. I can help."

Maybe it was what Mia had told him about Austen and Geiger being involved, but Bax had the distinct impression that Danny's offer was for more than headache relief. He stood up, made sure his notebook was tucked safely in his pocket. "Thanks, but I'll be fine."

Danny leaned back slowly, keeping his eye contact steady. "Anything I can do to be of assistance, Detective. I'm in suite 1510."

"I'll let you know." Bax got to the door and out into the garage, ninety-percent certain he'd been hit on. And ninety-percent certain Danny Austen had lied to him about the night of Geiger's murder.

MIA SMILED AT THE WOMAN standing at her station. She hadn't seen her before, but something told her that this woman wasn't a guest. There was an air of agitation about her, as if she'd just come from an accident or bad news.

It was in the way her long blondish hair rested on her shoulders, unkempt and slightly greasy. In the smudges of old makeup around her eyes, the paleness of her cheeks. Her blouse was silk, expensive, but her pants had seen better days.

"How can I help you?" Mia asked.

"I'm here for lunch with Piper Devon," she said. "But I'm early."

It was Sheila Geiger. No wonder she looked so distraught. "Would you like some tea to pass the time while I notify Ms. Devon?"

Mrs. Geiger looked at her sharply, as if she'd expected an argument. "If it comes with a shot of bourbon."

Mia turned to Allan at the front desk. "Could you take my calls for a bit, please?"

Allan nodded, and Mia came around her desk, slipping her earpiece into her pocket. "Let's get you comfortable," she said, leading Mrs. Geiger toward the bar.

They weren't open yet, but she knew Dahlia, the day bartender, was inside. While Mia looked for her, she made a quick call to Piper's office, letting her assistant know the situation.

A few minutes later, tea was being brewed and Mia sat across from the widow. "I'm so very sorry for your loss," she said.

"You know who I am?"

Mia smiled. "I was aware of the lunch engagement."

"So you know that someone from this hotel killed my husband."

"It must be devastating. How long were you married?"

"Eight years."

"That's a long time. Do you have children?"

Sheila shook her head. Some of the fire was gone from her eyes, but Mia knew she was treading close to the edge. "We meant to."

"It's so very sad. I hope you have someone to be with you. To help."

"My sister lives in Queens."

"That's good. Ah, here comes your tea."

Dahlia brought a pot of hot water and a box with an assortment of herbal teas along with two cups.

"Where's the bourbon?"

"Coming right up," Mia said, giving a nod to the bartender.

It was early yet, just past eleven in the morning. Mia was quite sure the bourbon was a bad idea, but she didn't want to agitate Mrs. Geiger further.

"They all thought he was such a bastard. Well he wasn't. He had a right to earn a living, just like anyone else. Those people, always complaining about the paparazzi, but they'd be pretty goddamn pissed if there was nobody wanting their pictures.

"I was the one who got the calls. Gerry was out working, so they'd call me. You know how all the photographers find out where the movie stars are gonna be? They call ahead, that's how. They call my house and leave messages. They're gonna be at Grand Union, at Hush, at all those bars all over the city. Then they spit on my husband for doing their dirty work."

"I had no idea," Mia said, sipping her Earl Grey.

Mrs. Geiger poured a very generous shot of bourbon into her cup. She didn't even look at the tea. "Those bastards. You ask that goddamn Danny Austen. He called my Gerry. Don't let him tell you different. He's got some secrets, that one. Just ask him about Mexico. Then he gets upset when Gerry finds out he goes both ways, you know? Damn bastard."

Danny Austen *was* bi. Mia had doubted it when Lorraine had suggested…but this confirmed the rumor, didn't it? Or was the tail wagging the dog? Maybe Danny wasn't bi at all. Maybe Gerry Geiger wanted to start something. Maybe that's what had gotten him killed. And there was that Mexico thing. Interesting.

She looked sharply at Mrs. Geiger, afraid she'd given something away. The woman was upset, distraught. And drunk. The bourbon Dahlia had brought wasn't her first. Probably wouldn't be her last. "Did Danny and your husband have an argument? I mean, just before…"

"Argument is putting it lightly. I told that cop that it was Danny who killed him. He didn't believe me, but that's because Danny Austen is a movie star. 'Cause he has all that money. But money won't get him off of a murder charge. Not if I have anything to say about it." Sheila leaned in, and Mia had to stop herself from turning away from the alcohol on the woman's breath. "He's a killer. He thinks I don't know. But I've got pictures."

"From that night?"

Sheila took a drink, then leaned in once more. Only she stopped as the bar door opened. One of Piper's assistants, not Lorraine this time, but Viv, was there as an escort to the meeting.

Mrs. Geiger didn't give Mia a second thought. Grabbing her teacup of bourbon, she left the bar, cursing up a storm.

Mia went back to her station, wishing like crazy she could just go find Bax. Sheila Geiger had the camera! That must mean she was tied to the murder somehow, right? How else would she have gotten the pictures? No, Sheila hadn't said they were from that night, so she'd better be careful what she told Bax. It was tempting to believe all she'd heard. Easy. Kind of how tempting it was to believe the tabloids.

She knew better. She would report what she'd heard but in a calm, clear way that didn't reflect her own opinions. It's what Piper would do.

Privately, however, she could think about what she'd heard. If Mrs. Geiger had the pictures from that night, what would that mean? That she'd killed him? Why would she want her husband dead, though? Sheila didn't work. Geiger was her meal ticket.

No, it made a lot more sense that this was about Austen's sex life. There were so many women madly in love with him, with his image, there's no way his career would stay intact if it was known he slept with men.

And what the heck was up with Mexico? A secret tryst? An affair gone bad?

She got her personal cell and hit Carlane's speed dial number. Her friend answered on the first ring.

"Have you heard any gossip about Danny Austen being bi?"

Carlane didn't miss a beat. "What? Who did you see?"

"No one. It might be completely untrue. Have you heard anything?"

"God, no. He's supposed to be the playboy of the western world."

"Okay, thanks."

"That's it? You're not even gonna tell me what you know?"

"I don't know anything. It was a rumor, nothing more. And the person saying it was drunk, so it's probably nothing."

"Damn, girl. My heart's racing. He can't be gay. It would just break my heart. I told you. All the good ones are married or gay. There's nothing left for us hetero gals."

"Don't panic. Seriously. Oh, wait, one more thing. Did Weinberg ever make a film in Mexico? With Bobbi or Danny or both?"

"Something about that rings a bell. Let me get back to you."

"I appreciate it, sweetie."

"Got a call. Talk to you later."

Mia hung up her phone and slipped it into her pocket. Sheila Geiger had been drunk and devastated. No reason to believe her, not even about the pictures. Although Mia would still tell Bax about their conversation.

She got a little shiver thinking about him. Was it not the most courtly gesture ever to meet her at the subway? He'd looked really good this morning, too. He'd worn dark jeans, an incredible soft, dark-green shirt and a leather jacket to die for.

Oh, man, she was in trouble. She'd worked herself into quite the orgasm last night and all from thinking about the possibilities. It had been so long since she'd had a crush, and this one was major. They had only three months before he was off to Colorado. But three months would be enough, if…

The problem was, did he want there to be something between them? It was hard to tell. She'd thought for sure he'd wanted to stay last night, but he'd walked away without a backward glance.

Maybe he wanted to get together, but since they were working together…

Oh, crap. That was it. He didn't want to risk the information. She'd basically become his informant. Maybe he thought things would get too messy if they pursued this…thing.

As far as she was concerned there was no cause for concern. They were both sensible and aware, and they both realized that the investigation had to come first. As long as they didn't get all crazy about things, they could still work together and have a little sex on the side. No harm, no foul.

Or not.

Why, out of all the men she'd met in months, did she find the detective so yummy? It was all wrong, and she'd do herself a big darn favor by forgetting about it. She had enough on her plate with her job, and now helping with the case. It was stupid to think of hooking up with Bax.

Stupid and addictive.

No, no. Mustn't linger in the land of make-believe. Focus on the work. On the great puzzle to be solved. Yes. The sooner they had the killer in custody, the sooner Detective Milligan would be…well, he'd be something. To find out what, she had to solve the crime. Fast.

"WHAT'S THE GOOD WORD?" Bax asked, fully prepared to hear nothing but bad words from Grunwald, who'd been dutifully following the chain of evidence as Bax was busy being jerked around by celebrities.

"We found some fibers, but nothing that's going to point to a killer. I'm still waiting on the official autopsy results but we know there wasn't a fight. Whoever did it came from behind. No defensive wounds."

"So we still don't know if it was a man or woman who killed him?"

"We'll know more once we get more results. I hear from the captain this one's going to hit the lab fast. What about you? Anyone looking good?"

"Everyone looks good. Too many fish in this barrel. I need to find out about the finances of the picture. How much the actors are getting paid. What kind of arrangements they have with Weinberg. I'm hearing noises that the film company is in trouble, too. So dig up what you can."

"Yeah, well, Miguel came back and he's assigned to the desk, so guess what he's gonna be doing?"

Bax laughed, knowing Miguel hated desk duty worse than anybody. "That'll teach him to wash his car."

"Good luck with those movie stars," Grunwald said.

"Yeah. I'll check in with you later." Bax disconnected and put his cell on his belt, wishing he could go back down to that nice little office in the basement of the hotel. He'd lock the door, turn off his phone and sleep until it was time to leave New York.

There was only one thing he'd miss, and it wasn't finding Geiger's killer.

An air horn went off down the street, signaling that the director had yelled cut. Most of today's scenes were being shot in the Hush garage, but they were also blocking part of East 41st Street, which was causing havoc with traffic.

He knew that the city made a fortune from these movie shoots, and that's why they were so willing to inconvenience the denizens of midtown, but man, what a mess.

Bobbi Tamony had blown him off twice, and that was going to stop right now. He didn't give a shit about her schedule or her temperament. He'd had it with these prima donnas.

With a curse, he pushed himself off the side of the building. It was just past noon, and if the first assistant director was to be believed, the filming would stop for lunch any minute.

"Bax!"

He turned at the sound of Mia's voice. All of a sudden he wasn't so tired. There she was, coming out of the big glass door, rushing toward him in her black tux. The smile on her face put one on his.

"Are you swamped?" she asked.

"No."

"Really? You have some time?" She looked past him, to the big barricades holding back the pedestrians, the off-duty beat cops making an extra dime. Past them were trailers and equipment and a bunch of crew people scurrying to and fro as if they were doing something important.

"I'm all yours," he said.

She flushed enough for him to catch it on her cheeks. "Great. Where can we go that's private?"

He thought about taking her down to the office he'd been given, but he wanted her away from Hush. If he could have, he'd take her far away, say, the Cloisters or at least Central Park. Then it hit him. "Come with me."

She walked along beside him, and the urge to take her hand was strong. Really strong. But he was on the clock and so was she. Hadn't he just lectured himself about this very thing?

"Where are we going?"

"I think I have somewhere nice and quiet and private," he said. "I have to check, though."

They walked past the barricade into the heart of the location. It wasn't difficult to find the AD. She was standing in the middle of the street, papers in one hand, a walkie-talkie in the other.

He touched Mia's arm. "Wait here. I'll be right back."

She nodded as she stared at all the equipment and chairs and the thrum of activity.

The business with the AD took only a few minutes. Then he was back at Mia's side. "Come on," he said, pleased that things were going to work out, at least for the next hour. He didn't want anyone from the film company or Hush knowing he was using Mia as his go-between.

He led her to the garage, to the row of trailers and motor homes. When he got to the fourth huge motor home, the only one without a name plate, he opened the door and waited for Mia to climb the four steps.

"What's this?" she asked.

"It's what movie stars use instead of port-a-potties."

She whistled as she got a load of the five-star accommodations. It wasn't exactly like Danny Austen's, but it was close.

"This is like a suite at the hotel," she said, running her hand over the top of the white leather armchair. "Are you sure it's okay that we're here?"

"No one's using this one, at least for today. I checked."

She looked at him with a hint of wicked in her big dark eyes. "So no one's gonna come knocking?"

He shook his head.

Mia approached him slowly, her fingertips trailing over the table. "I've got a whole hour until I have to get back to work."

She was tiny next to him. His hands could fit around her waist. The top of her head didn't even come up to his chin and she smelled like a soft, sweet flower. But the look in her eyes was bold as brass.

Wanting her swamped him, made him lift his hand to pull her close. To kiss her would ease the ache that had been there since they'd met. It would let him sleep again. But in his dreams, he hadn't stopped at a kiss.

Bax forced himself to take a step back. To make it really clear that this was business and nothing more. It didn't matter that she wanted it. That he wanted it.

Man, his job sucked.

6

OKAY, SO SHE'D MISJUDGED the situation. It happened. No big deal, right?

Turning away from Bax, who'd done everything but send up a flare to let her know that he wasn't interested in anything beyond a work relationship, she gathered her pride and her wits about her as she sat in the chair next to the table. No chance of him getting close from this position. "Sheila Geiger came to the hotel this morning. She had some interesting things to say."

Bax nodded as his gaze moved from her to the couch back to her then to the other single chair across from the table. That's where he chose to sit. "You talked to her yourself?"

"Yes. In the bar. She was early and I took her to get some tea."

"She didn't seem like the tea type to me."

"Yes, well, sometimes our initial impressions aren't all that accurate, are they."

"Point taken."

She hadn't meant to get snarky with him. Using her most practiced smile, she leaned in, making sure her body language was friendly, open. Not in the least sexual. "Anyway, she's pretty sure that Danny Austen killed her husband."

Bax blinked at her as if something didn't compute. He'd

already said he thought Sheila wasn't unhappy that her husband was dead, and Sheila had admitted she'd told him about her suspicions, so why was this revelation troubling him? Then it occurred to her. She was grinning at him as if she'd just told him he'd won a stuffed bunny. She ditched the big smile and eased back about ten degrees. "She also said that she thinks it's because Gerry knew that Danny bats for both teams."

"Shit," Bax said.

"What?"

"Nothing. Just that I think it's true."

"That Danny killed Geiger?"

"No. That Danny is bisexual."

"Well, I wouldn't exactly take Sheila Geiger's word as gospel."

He shook his head. "Actually, I'm pretty sure that Austen hit on me this morning."

"What?"

"I was thinking maybe I got it wrong, but now that two sources have confirmed it—"

"He hit on you? How?"

"It's not important. What else did—"

"Oh, no. Come on. I'm not going to tell anyone. What did he say?"

Bax looked flustered. He scratched his head, making little tufts of dark hair stand up, and he didn't meet her eyes. "I had a headache. He offered to help me with it."

"Holy crap."

"I said no."

She laughed. "I wasn't suggesting that you didn't. I've just always thought, you know, Danny Austen. He's legendary."

"But is he a killer?"

"I haven't finished about Sheila."

He leaned forward, looking pleased that they were talking once more about murder.

"She said she had pictures."

"From that night?"

"Don't know. I asked, but then someone came in. She never answered me."

"Did she give you any specifics about the pictures?"

"She implied they were of Danny and someone else. A man. She said they would prove that he was the killer."

"Unless they show him with the murder weapon, or actually killing Geiger, I doubt that. But they sure could point to motive."

"If she's telling the truth."

"You didn't believe her?"

She hadn't wanted to tell him this, not after being such a snot with that comment, but she had to. "She was drunk."

"When?"

"This morning. When she got to the hotel. It's crazy, too, because she was going to lunch with Piper and Trace."

"Trace is the attorney, right?"

"Yes. Piper's husband."

"Sheila knew that. Knew she was meeting with counsel."

"Maybe not. I don't know. Even so, it seems like awfully poor judgment."

He leaned back again. "The alcohol must be a considerable problem, then. She has a lot on the line. A lot to lose."

"Or she's really devastated by the loss of her husband."

Bax shook his head even as he said, "I suppose so."

"You don't believe her?"

"I'd have to see the evidence for myself."

"Can't you get a search warrant? Get all the cameras from their house?"

"I don't know. We'll have to see if a judge will get on board. But there's no guarantee, even if we swept the house, that the pictures would be there."

Mia stood up, anxious now to leave this very private and inviting motor home. But she couldn't go just yet. Not until she knew for sure.

She remembered a lesson her mother had taught her long ago—don't ask a question if you're not prepared to hear the answer. But she was prepared. Better to get things out on the table. Deal with what was, not what she wished could be. "Bax?"

"Yeah?"

"I don't mean to make you uncomfortable or anything, but I got some pretty strong vibes before. About us."

He met her gaze. "You did, huh?"

"Was I crazy?"

Bax closed his eyes for a second, then shook his head slowly. "No, you weren't."

"Ah."

He stood up. Came close. "But here's the thing—"

"You don't have to explain," she said. "I just—"

"I do. There are some propriety issues as well as some legal issues."

"I'm twenty-eight, for heaven's sake."

"Not that kind of legal," he said, smiling at her. "We made an agreement last night. You're an informant. You may have to testify, and if that came to pass, and then it came out that we—that I—"

"Oh."

"So, it's not that I don't want to."

She stepped back, not sure if she needed to discuss this any further. "It's for the best. You're leaving. I have so much to do with the hotel and everything—"

"Right, right. Those are all really good reasons."

She backed up some more, almost to the door. "I'd better—"

"Sure. Yes. And thanks for that information. Helpful. Good."

"No problem. All part of the service. As informant, I mean."

He opened his mouth, then shut it again. His gaze went down to the notebook in his hand, and she slipped out the door.

BOBBI TAMONY WAS in her motor home, and by this time, Bax was no longer impressed. It all felt foolish to him, a giant game that half the world had bought into, but that really meant nothing. All pretense, no substance.

He'd seen a lot of Bobbi's movies in his time and had enjoyed them for the most part, but she was just a suspect. A suspect with two very small, very yappy dogs that had the run of the trailer.

"Can I get you something? A drink? A snack?"

"No, thank you," he said, sitting in the big chair by the door, just as he had with Danny. Bax eyed the couch, wishing for the hundredth time that he hadn't been such a fool with Mia. It wasn't that he'd changed his mind about what he could and couldn't do, but he was damn sure a smarter man would have handled things more adroitly. He'd embarrassed her. Embarrassed himself. And damn it, he still wanted her.

He'd known her what, a couple of days? How was it possible he liked her so intensely? That he couldn't shake the feel of her, the scent of her?

This was new for him. The last woman he'd been serious about, Carol, hadn't bamboozled him like this. They'd started as friends in the academy and the relationship had progressed. They'd decided that it would be good to live together, and that had been pretty good for five whole years.

Then she'd met someone. A fellow cop Bax knew casually, someone he'd never have imagined with Carol. He was one of those manly men. Hunted, fished, worked out with great big dumbbells. To the best of Bax's knowledge, it had never occurred to him to pick up a book. Carol seemed happy with him, though, so there it was. He used to miss her. Now, he only thought about her when they ran into each other through the job.

This thing with Mia, though, there was none of the distance he'd had with Carol. It was as if she'd bypassed his logic circuits, hitting him straight in the emotions. Not smart. Not when they were both involved with a big case like this one.

"Did you want to ask me some questions, Detective?"

Shit. "Yes, I do." He pulled out his notebook and pen. "First, why don't you tell me about your relationship with Gerry Geiger."

"Relationship? We didn't have one, other than him being a pain in my ass."

"In what way?"

She smiled, and he thought of how different it was to see that famous grin life-sized instead of on a movie screen. "He was no different from all the other stalkerazzis.

Always looking to get the most unflattering pictures, the most compromising positions. The uglier the better."

"Did he catch you in any compromising positions?"

"Lots of times. I'd like to tell you my life has been so pure there was nothing for him to catch, but that would be a crock. I've partied with the best of them, or perhaps I should say the worst. In fact, it was Gerry who managed to get a copy of my mug shot when I was busted for that DUI in L.A."

"Did you and he have any discussions about that?"

"No, Detective, we didn't. We had no discussions whatsoever. Come here, baby. Come on."

Bax bit back a sigh as the women segued from the interview to getting her tiny dog on her lap. Then he waited for a couple of minutes as the dog, nestled under her considerable cleavage, barked at him. Bobbi didn't seem to mind. In fact, she seemed a little calmer after the dog finally shut up.

"As for the night he was murdered, I left the nightclub set at a quarter to eleven. You can check with the AD who signed me out. I then went to my room, took a very long bath and went to bed."

"Anyone who can confirm that?"

"The pet concierge, Mercy I believe her name is, brought the babies to my room."

"Do you remember what time?"

"No. Sometime after eleven. After that, no one can vouch for me. Sorry."

"Do you think someone from the film killed him?"

She didn't seem the least shaken by his question. "Very possibly. He wasn't a nice man, Detective. He was rude, pushy, obnoxious. His lifeblood was our misery."

"And yet, according to Mrs. Geiger, you called on him to take pictures when it suited you."

"Look, sweetie, I didn't make the calls myself," she said with a slight roll of her eyes. "Oscar has people who do that kind of thing, not me."

"So you never actually spoke to Mrs. Geiger."

"God, no. But from what I hear, she's quite the lush. Even Gerry Geiger had had enough of that one. I heard he was getting ready to leave her."

"How did you hear that?"

"Was it Nan? Maybe not. You have to understand, Detective—do you have a first name? That detective bit is getting old."

"We're almost done. Was it Nan Collins who told you that Geiger was leaving his wife?"

"I don't recall, honestly. It was just one of those rumors on the set. You know how those are."

"No. How are they?"

She smiled, clearly not appreciating his humor.

"That's it?" he asked.

"That's it."

"You'll let me know if you think of anything else, yes?"

Her smile became even less charming. Perhaps he should have let her call him Bax.

"I'll rush to find you if I think of another thing."

He stood, causing the dogs to get hysterical yet again, and then he was outside in the warm June afternoon. He needed to type up his notes, call Grunwald, although he was no closer to a suspect. But attention had to be paid to the protocols.

Besides, once he was inside, he could check room service records and find out about the pet concierge. Jeez, hotels had certainly changed a lot. Or maybe he was just a hopeless hick, destined for backwoods motels.

As he entered the hotel lobby, his gaze went straight to the front desk, to Mia. She didn't see him, engrossed as she was on the computer and her phone. He watched her for a long while, probably too long. She typed and talked with a smile that he knew now was genuine. Not like Bobbi Tamony, or any of those movie people. None of those actors could hold a candle to Mia. She was beautiful, wickedly bright— Bax closed his eyes. This was not good.

In fact, it was humiliating. Thirty-six years old, and he was moony over a slip of a girl. Jesus. Pretty soon he'd be writing her name on the back of his notebook.

He turned around and walked outside, stretching his legs for the first time that day. Thinking about this situation.

First of all, he was leaving. He'd already been accepted at Boulder and there was nothing for him in New York, so it wasn't optional. Second, she wasn't leaving. Mia had scored herself an incredible job, and she wasn't about to give that up for the likes of him. Third, he was really, really tired. That was probably what all this insanity was about. He'd get a good night's sleep and things would go back to normal.

This was not the way he did things.

He was on a case, for God's sake. A high-profile murder. What, did he think he could skate just because he'd turned in his resignation? As long as he was on the damn clock, he would put his entire energy on the job, not on his dick.

Only, it wasn't just his dick.

Shit.

"You have a minute, Mia?"

"Sure. What's up?"

It was Mercy, the pet concierge at Hush and one of Mia's favorite people here at the hotel. She was shy and sweet, and they'd had great talks about crazy guests and their pets, not to mention all the hotel gossip. They met for drinks or dinner whenever they could.

She seemed distracted, which was understandable. They'd had an extraordinary number of pets recently, all of them wanting the kind of specialized services Hush was famous for. Home-baked treats, massages, walks of course, and playtime in the PetQuarters. Mercy had even hired special help to get through the month as most of her personal time was spent caring for Bobbi Tamony's two Chihuahuas.

"You were with that policeman this morning, right?"

"Detective Milligan? Yeah, I was helping him with some details about the case."

"Uh-huh, anyway, I don't know if I should bother him— No, it's nothing. Sorry, I'll leave you alone."

"Wait. Don't go. What was it you wanted to tell him?"

Mercy also wore the Hush uniform, but her pink bow tie had little black puppies on it. She had bigger pockets on her jacket, too, to hold all the biscuits. What made her look completely adorable though was that she wore her long blond hair up in a ponytail, held there with a big pink bow that matched her tie. So cute. But Mia could tell she wasn't her usual perky self.

"I don't know. It's probably nothing." Mercy stepped closer to the desk. "It just that when I went up last night to deliver the pups, I could tell Bobbi had been crying."

"Was anyone with her?"

"No, but she was acting really odd. She shoved a bunch of stuff under her blanket when I walked into the room."

"It could have just been, you know, Hush stuff."

Mercy waved her hand. "Oh, heck no. She leaves her vibrators out on display on top of her night tables. She was really bothered by something. I asked if I could do anything and she said no, but…"

"What?"

"I saw the guy that was murdered coming out of her room that night."

"The night he was killed?"

Mercy nodded. "I have no idea what he was doing there, or if it means anything. You think I should tell him? The detective?"

"Yeah. I think so. It could mean something."

"All right. I'll find him before he goes home. Thanks."

"No problem. Let me know if there's anything else you think of. I mean, it's probably easier for me to catch the detective."

"Uh-huh," Mercy gave her a look that said she wasn't fooled in the least. "As soon as this madness is over, you and I will have ourselves a talk." She leaned over the edge of the desk. "He is pretty damn hot."

Mia felt a blush heat her cheeks. Lucky for her, the phone rang. "Concierge, this is Mia, how may I help you?"

Mercy shook her head as she left and Mia was quite certain that if Mercy, who was far more intuitive about puppies than people, knew about her thing for Bax, then the entire staff at Hush knew as well. Great.

7

"YOU'RE HERE."

Bax nodded then got up from the pony wall in the Hush garage. "I wanted to make sure you got home safely."

Mia approached him, a little bit thrilled that he was here and a little bit leery as to why. "You didn't have to. The paps don't seem to care that much about me today."

"Fools."

"Oh," she said, but she didn't think he heard her. This was so odd. It was like some elaborate dance but she didn't know the steps. He comes close, he backs away, he tells her it's all about the job, then says, "Fools." Not fair. And still, she was drawn to him. Terribly so.

She touched the sleeve of his leather jacket. As June was coming into its own the days and nights were becoming warmer. Soon that leather would be too much for the season and he'd put the jacket away. She bet he looked great in a T-shirt. "It's nice of you."

"I would have preferred driving you home, but all I can do tonight is see you to the subway. I've got to go to the precinct."

"Did Mercy find you?"

"Neither mercy nor grace, unfortunately. I've been stuck with sloth and greed all day."

Mia grinned. "I meant Mercy, the pet concierge."

"Right. Uh, no. No, she didn't."

"She told me a couple of things you should know. Come on, walk me to the subway and I'll fill you in."

He didn't take her hand, but she thought he wanted to. She sure did. Instead, she did what she knew was safe. Told him all she could remember about her conversation with Mercy. She was terribly professional and when they were standing at the subway steps and he looked at her with his deep brown eyes, she melted like an ice cream cone in summer. At least on the inside.

She thought about him all the way to Brooklyn Heights. Even the murder didn't stand a chance of chasing Bax away. As she climbed into bed at ten-thirty, she had to admit it. He wasn't just a crush. No crush had ever made her feel like this. She was a goner.

DESPITE THE FACT that it was almost lunchtime, Mia didn't do the sensible thing and relax in the break room. Oh, no. She decided to steal away to the trailers and deliver a rather large fruit and muffin basket that had been left for Danny Austen. Maybe she could get him talking. He might open up to her more than he would to a police detective, right?

She made a quick restroom stop just to make sure she looked her best, then hauled the basket from behind the desk and headed out.

The security guard at the exit was sweet, holding the door for her and asking if he could be of help, but this was something she needed to do alone.

The garage was pretty empty, which meant this trip was probably a waste of time. Usually, when there was no one by the trailers it meant they were all on the set. Oh, well. She would still deliver the basket.

She had to switch hands twice before she found his particular motor home because the basket was so heavy. Thankfully, she wouldn't have to carry it much further. Resting on the step in front of the door, she knocked. "Mr. Austen? I have a delivery."

She waited. Thought about breaking down and buying something from the vending machines in the break room. Something naughty.

Another knock. "Mr. Austen? Delivery."

She waited for half a mo, then tried the door. It was open. She'd seen the way the movie people were with these so-called trailers. They were like offices, and people seemed to go in and out without much concern. Still, she poked her head in. Nothing.

With a push and a heave, she went inside, amazed again at the opulence. She could have easily lived there. Heck, they could have taken off the wheels and she'd have been happy.

Mia put the basket on the table. Walking toward the back of the motor home, she touched the marble countertops. They didn't seem like a veneer. One thing she hadn't seen in the empty trailer was the bathroom.

She went back and opened the first door, but that was just a closet. Then she opened the second door.

And screamed.

Danny Austen, naked as the day he was born, was in a very tiny shower with another very naked man. They were both all soapy and foamy, which made sense because there was no water running to wash them off.

She jumped back and slammed the door shut.

The stupid thing bounced and flew open again, giving her an even more unfortunate view.

One more time, she shut the door, catching it this time with both hands.

She was out of that trailer almost as quickly as Piper was going to fire her.

THERE WAS NO GOOD TIME to read a tabloid. Bax realized that profound truth immediately, but there was also no turning back.

The cover in his hand had all the bold printed scandals that would fit, but he was only interested in the central picture. Bobbi Tamony, dressed in something gold and slinky, was sitting at a banquette, her head bent over a large mirror. There was a rolled-up bill at her nose through which she was snorting what looked like several hundred dollars' worth of cocaine.

The photograph wasn't credited and the date given was the unhelpful *sometime last week*. Still, he couldn't help but wonder if this picture was worthy of murder. How had the paper gotten the photo? From which paparazzo?

The last thing he wanted to do was talk to those cretins. One was worst than the next, yanking out their First Amendment rights at the drop of a hat, despite the fact it was clear they had no idea what the First Amendment said.

But what choice did he have? The paparazzi were Geiger's people. This afternoon Bax had three of them lined up, the most interesting of whom was Henry Toth. According to his compatriots, Toth and Geiger were rivals, not just with work, but on a personal level.

That wasn't for another half hour, though, so Bax went back to the magazines. He really hated that he'd spent perfectly good money on this crap. That, in fact, he had a whole stack of tabloids staring at him. He cared nothing about which stars' diets were now disasters. Which plastic surgeries had gone horribly wrong. Or what starlet was the latest to be dumped.

He also hated that he'd been read the riot act last night by the captain. Not that he was doing anything wrong, just that he wasn't doing the right things faster. Much faster.

Seemed Oscar Weinberg had friends. Lots of them. In very high places. Who didn't seem terribly concerned that a paparazzo had been killed. In fact, the subtext had been that the killer had done a public service.

On the other side of the coin were the tabloids themselves, rallied to a cause that had more to do with sensational headlines than actual concern, but a cause nonetheless that made the NYPD look bad.

Why, then, was it taking him so long to find the murderer?

He hadn't bothered to answer the captain's questions. The captain hadn't become the captain because he was a stupid man. He understood exactly why things were moving at a snail's pace. He also understood that by giving Bax grief, he was absolving himself of any guilt associated with the case. He could happily move on to the next crisis, leaving Bax to take whatever blame might come. Would come.

Bax sighed as he picked up the next tabloid on the pile. It too had a picture of interest on the cover. Not of Bobby Tamony, but of Danny Austen. Nothing about his sexual preferences unless you counted partying with a barely eighteen-year-old starlet.

Something about the picture… He went back to the

front page featuring Bobbi Tamony, then put the two magazines side by side. There, in the background in both pictures, was the same woman. Nan Collins, the glorified extra. There was no mistaking her, despite the blurriness of the photos.

She wore a cut-down-to-there blouse, the same blouse in both shots. In one picture, she looked directly at the camera. In the other, she looked to the right. A man might surmise the picture had been taken on the same night.

Perhaps Bobbi and Danny had been at the same club? It didn't look like the Hush hotel bar. The décor was all wrong. Mia would know. She might just know something about the woman, too. He'd better go—

He put the brakes on. He needed to be careful about her. Yes, she was an excellent resource, but to depend on her and her gossip too much could lead him to unwarranted conclusions. It was so easy to believe everything she said, even after her own admissions that she was repeating rumors. He liked her. He wanted her to be right. It was a recipe for mistakes the case couldn't afford.

So was this an instance when going to Mia was justified? Or was he making excuses to be near her?

The answer was both. She was an excellent source, and so far the information she'd given him was all worthy of being checked out. He also wanted to see her.

He wasn't the type to feel lonely. Not when there was a book to be read. But last night? His apartment had felt empty, and he'd picked up three different books, none of which had held his attention.

He closed the office door behind him and went to the lobby.

SHE KNEW BAX WAS THERE even before she looked up. Something in the air had shifted, or maybe it was a new kind of personal radar attuned to his scent, his molecules.

His smile made her blush and she finished up her call as quickly as she could.

"I'm sorry about this morning," he said.

"What for?"

"I wanted to meet you out there, but—"

"It's okay. I appreciate the thought."

He touched the edge of her cuff briefly, then pulled back. "I've got some pictures, some tabloid shots I'd like you to look at when you have a break."

"I can come now."

"No, you're working. And I have some paps to talk to as soon as I finish with Bobbi Tamony. Has Weinberg come back?"

She shook her head. "He should be back sometime this evening. We're getting his suite ready for him."

"Okay. I just…"

"What?"

"Nothing. If I'm not in the office, give me a call. You have my cell number, right?"

"Yep. And you have mine."

"That I do. I should call you just to hear that ring of yours."

"It's distinctive."

"It's Wagner."

"And what's wrong with Wagner?"

"Not a thing." He slapped the top of the desk lightly. "See you later, huh?"

"Wouldn't miss it."

As she watched him walk away she tried to get her heartbeat to slow. He looked good. Jeans again, which she liked much, much better than the brown pants. A white button-down shirt. A black jacket, nothing heavy, maybe linen or cotton. It was a good combination. Especially with his rebellious hair and his dark eyes.

Man, she had it bad.

He'd mentioned tabloids. She should run to the gift shop, but no, the front desk was busy. As long as she had a minute, though, she could call her expert. Carlane would have all the latest rags already, and if there was anything about the murder, her friend would know.

She wondered if she should tell Carlane about what she'd seen in Danny's trailer. No, that was private information. Very private.

Mia was still amazed she hadn't gotten fired. But then, Piper wasn't in-house, so maybe Danny was waiting to express his outrage personally. It was quite possible this would be her very last day at Hush. That would break her heart. But she'd deal. She'd have to.

In the meantime, maybe there was one more thing she could do to help Bax before she was kicked out on her keister.

"YOU SAW THE PICTURE, I assume?"

Bax walked over to Bobbi, who was sitting in a chair that had her name on it. They were on the Madison Avenue sidewalk and the camera was set up in the little coffee shop where he and Mia had first had dinner.

There were several occupied chairs around them, but Danny Austen's was empty. As was Peter Eccles's. Bax pulled Austen's chair closer to Bobbi and sat down. "Want to tell me about it?"

"If I tell you it was cold medicine, will you believe me?"

"No."

"Will it matter?"

"Only if that picture is what got Geiger killed."

She shifted on her chair, crossing one famously long, slender leg over the other. Her outfit today seemed pretty casual. A denim skirt, sandals, a little sleeveless T. He wondered if the clothes were hers or if she was in costume.

"I don't know who took that picture, Detective."

"They let a bunch of paps into those nightclubs, do they?"

"For all I know, the bartender had a camera in his cell phone."

"Right."

"You think I want the world to see me like that?"

"You're on the cover."

"You're a cynical man, Milligan."

"I'm a peach. It's the job that makes me cynical."

Bobbi smiled. "You know what? I believe you. I wish I could be of more help. I don't remember much from that night."

"What night would that be?"

"Four nights ago? Five? It's hard to recall."

"I'll bet. You remember a woman standing behind you? Tall redhead? Name of Nan Collins?"

She shook her head. "If she was there, I didn't notice."

"Was Danny partying with you that night?"

"Danny? We don't tend to hang out after work. You know how that is."

He could see he wasn't going to get anything useful from her. He'd do better waiting to talk to Mia. Maybe that pet concierge was available. Or maybe he should get on the horn with the tabloids, not that they'd tell him anything without being compelled by the courts.

"Detective?"

He got up, looked around for Austen or the director. Neither one was on the street. But shit, were there ever crowds. Tons of people held back by the barricades. Lots of off-duty cops getting some sweet moonlighting money. "Yeah?"

"I do remember someone who was partying with me that night."

"Oh?"

"Our dear director. And I don't think he was having a very good time."

Bax nodded. It was probably a misdirection, probably nothing. But because she'd said it, he'd do his damnedest to get to the truth. Which was funny, considering. "Have a good day, Ms. Tamony."

"You, too, Bax."

YOLANDA WAS GETTING Oscar Weinberg's suite ready, which wasn't a simple thing to do. Mia had no business interrupting. No business being there at all. But did that stop her?

"Yolanda?"

"Hello Miss Mia."

"How are you?"

"I'm fine, thank you. Just getting this room ready."

"I came to check on a few things, if you don't mind."

Yolanda, who was an excellent maid and a very nice person, stepped away from the door. "No problem, Miss Mia. You do what you need to. Let me know if I can help."

Mia nodded as she walked inside. Oh, man, she was stepping close to the line here. Okay, over the line. Yes, she was going to check to make sure Mr. Weinberg's pillows were perfect, but mostly she was going to snoop.

Yolanda had disappeared into the master bedroom, so Mia had the living room to herself. First thing she did was go to the to the big closet. There were clothes in there, and two suitcases. With her heart racing, Mia checked both cases. Empty. She felt for pockets on the jackets and came up with nothing there, either.

Okay, second bedroom. As she hurried, the theme music from *Mission Impossible* played in her head even as she told herself this was not a game. If she was caught here, she could lose her job. On the other hand, she was probably already on the cut list, so what the hell.

The second bedroom looked pristine and had already been turned down. Mia had no idea if Weinberg ever used the second bed, but it was ready if he wanted to.

The closet in there was empty and Mia was just about to shut the door when she realized that there was a mirror on the side wall. She'd been in every suite in the hotel, but she couldn't remember seeing a mirror like this one.

She stepped inside the closet. The mirror had a wooden frame, very polished. It was maybe two feet long and four feet wide. The more she thought about it, the more sure she became that this mirror wasn't standard.

She looked out to make sure she was alone, then peered at the side of the mirror. It was at least two inches in depth, which made her think that perhaps it wasn't for looking in so much as it was for hiding things.

With held breath, she pulled on the left side, then the right. Nothing budged. She let her fingers trail around the entire frame. She felt a break in the upper right corner. Tugging did nothing, so instead, she pushed. Something gave, although it didn't open.

The push gave her hope, though. She had a friend in

Toronto who built secret-compartment boxes, and with her love of puzzles, Mia had found them endlessly fascinating. The important part of puzzle boxes was that at least two mechanisms had to be manipulated concurrently to release a catch.

Mia stood on tiptoe to study the break in the frame. She tugged, pushed and lifted in every way she could think of when the frame popped open.

Her sigh was loud in the little closet and she'd already stayed too long, so she swung the mirror out, expecting jewelry or drugs or both.

What she got were memory cards. The kind that went inside digital cameras. Lots and lots of memory cards.

She picked one up and saw that it was 256K. She turned the little electronic gizmo over and whoa, there it was. Initials written in a very small hand. BT.

She put that card back and picked up another, this one from a different stack. The initials on this one, PE.

In the next few minutes, she found many initials she couldn't decipher. And many she could.

DA for Danny Austen.

GG for Gerry Geiger.

SG as in Sheila Geiger?

PD which might or might not be Piper Devon.

Mia's already racing pulse went zooming out of control. She wasn't exactly sure what she'd found, but she knew, just knew, it was something important. She couldn't even conceive of how many pictures were stored here. Thousands upon thousands.

Did one of these cards hold the key to Geiger's murder? Was the killer none other than Oscar Weinberg?

She thought about taking the card with GG on the back,

but she just couldn't. There was no way she could justify stealing so blatantly. God forbid Weinberg kept an inventory and discovered the theft. Where would his finger point? Right at Yolanda, that's where.

No, she and Bax would have to come up with another way to get these memory cards into evidence.

"Miss Mia?"

Mia jumped what felt like ten feet, then slammed the mirror closed. Thankfully, Yolanda was still in the other room. "Yes, Yolanda?"

"I finished the bedroom. You want to come check?"

"Thanks. I'll be right there."

THE PET FACILITIES WERE on the 20th floor, adjacent to the elaborate and expansive spa. Bax had to admit he was curious about the pet concierge. Dog walking? Puppy sitting? He'd never been to a hotel that had pet facilities, unless you count lawns. Of course, it had been years since he'd had a dog. That was one of his first priorities when he got to Boulder. He'd grown up with pets and he missed that. The companionship, the exercise. He'd be able to hike to his heart's content in Boulder, a trusty mutt beside him.

He pushed the door open and walked into a world that was as outside his own reality as a movie set.

PetQuarters had a front desk, just like downstairs, barring his view to the pets, and a very attractive young woman wearing a modified Hush uniform holding one of Bobbi Tamony's yappy dogs. He knew it was Bobbi's because of the way his hackles rose hearing that bark.

"May I help you?"

"I'm looking for Mercy."

The young woman sighed. "Aren't we all."

Bax laughed, but cut it short as the woman's expression told him she meant that quite literally. He coughed, hoping to let the moment slide.

"Mercy should have been back ten minutes ago. And Eddy had to leave for class, and then Ms. Tamony came to deliver her dogs, and well, I'm kind of on my own, but if I can be of any assistance?"

"No, it's fine. You have your hands full. I'll come back later."

"Would you like Mercy to give you a call? I can take your number."

"No, but thanks." He was curious about the parts of the puppy hotel he couldn't see, but he'd explore it later. For now, he'd go see if Mia had some time for him. She'd been too busy a few minutes ago. He'd been tempted to just watch her as she did her thing, but he'd nixed that plan.

He waited around in the reception area, hoping Mercy would show up. Thinking about his interview with Henry Toth.

According to Toth, who he'd have mistaken for a pan-handler if it hadn't been for his very expensive cameras, Geiger had some very tight connections with both Bobbi and Danny Austen. That he knew for a fact that Geiger was tipped off by someone working for Weinberg. And that Gerry Geiger had just bought himself a hell of a nice duplex in Little Italy.

Toth also suggested that Geiger was more than a little fed up with his wife's drinking.

The sad thing? That bunch of schoolyard gossip was the most he'd gotten from any of the paparazzi so far. They were a tight-lipped bunch of bottom-feeders.

It didn't appear that Mercy the pet concierge was coming back anytime soon. As Bax rounded the corner toward the elevator he spotted a man in the spa window. He was hefty, balding, wearing a robe.

Bax went into the spa's reception area, but the man was gone. There were two ladies looking at some cosmetics, one man who Bax had seen on some TV show, and the women behind the desk.

The woman closest to him, a little older than her compatriot, smiled at him. "May I help you?"

He pulled out his wallet and flashed his badge. "I need to know if Oscar Weinberg is inside the facility."

"Yes, sir, he is."

"Great. Which room?"

"He's in the middle of a procedure at the moment."

"I don't mind."

She looked at her coworker, then back at him. "Can you give me a minute, please? I honestly don't know how to handle this situation and I'd like to ask someone."

"Is this the only exit?"

"Yes, sir."

"Take your time."

While she called whoever she called, Bax picked up one of the brochures from the counter. The services were vast and expensive, and some were downright odd. Hot stones? Oxygen facials? What he knew about spas could fit on the end of his pen, but he was once again, as he was so often lately, impressed by what the rich would buy. He was sure they would defend the spa services as crucial to their health and happiness. Hell, maybe they were right.

"Officer?"

He put the brochure down. "That's Detective."

"Sorry. Detective. I can take you to see Mr. Weinberg now."

"Great."

She led him inside the spa proper, down a long hallway. It smelled good, like trees, and the lighting was low. Music played softly in the background. New-age stuff, of course, but it hit all the right marks for a spa.

After a few turns, she stopped in front of a closed door. A gentle knock was followed almost immediately by the door opening a crack.

"I've got a client."

The woman nodded. "The detective needs to speak to Mr. Weinberg."

"He's still got half an hour to go."

Bax moved closer to the door. "I'll be busy in a half an hour."

"I checked with Piper's office," the woman whispered. "We have to let him in."

The massage therapist was tall and wiry, not bulging with muscles as Bax would have thought. He looked strong though, strong and pissed. The one thing that did match Bax's preconceived notions was the uniform. All-white T-shirt, slacks and shoes. Clean. Antiseptic.

After a meaningful shrug, the therapist stepped back.

Bax thanked the nice woman and went inside the even darker room.

Turns out it wasn't dark enough.

Oscar Weinberg lay naked on the massage table. Face up. With no sheet covering any part of his large body.

Bax almost turned around and walked out, but his

personal discomfort couldn't possibly be worse than Weinberg's, so why not go for it?

"What the hell is going on, Larry?"

"I'm sorry, Mr. Weinberg. I was told to let him in."

Weinberg looked Bax over. "Who the fuck are you?"

Bax took out his badge, making sure Oscar saw his holster as he did so. "Detective Milligan."

"This can't wait?"

"I figured I better catch you when I could. With that private jet and all."

"Did I say I wanted you to stop the massage?"

That was to Larry, of course, who hopped to it.

Bax had no idea what Larry was in fact massaging as he was focusing one hundred percent on Weinberg's face. "When did you get back to the hotel?"

"About an hour ago."

"And the first thing you wanted was a massage?"

"Is that what you came here to talk about?"

Score one for the naked guy. "Tell me about your relationship with Geiger."

"There was no relationship. We used Geiger on occasion to take pictures. We paid him. All above board, nothing special."

"Was he on the clock the night of his death?"

"No. He was not."

"You're sure about that?" Bax didn't wait for a response. "When was the last time you did hire him?"

"I'll have to find out, Detective. It's not something I keep at the forefront. Especially with Geiger. The man was an ass. Rude, greedy. He was one of the worst."

"Then why use him?"

"He got the job done. He was useful."

"What was Geiger doing in Peter Eccles's suite?"

Weinberg rolled his eyes as if the question was too difficult to bear. "You'd have to ask Peter."

"According to some reliable sources you've got a lot riding on this picture. The last four movies you produced haven't done very well."

"Reliable sources? Please, Detective. You should know by now that you can't always believe what you read in the papers."

"I imagine it's costing a lot. Austen and Tamony don't come cheap."

"We won't be selling off our company jet anytime soon."

"Why do you think someone wanted Geiger dead?"

"He probably took a picture he shouldn't have. Honestly, Detective, I wouldn't know. The lives of the paparazzi are of little consequence to me."

Bax was about to pepper him with yet another question, despite the fact that the naked guy was turning out to be pretty imperturbable, but then Oscar took hold of Larry's left arm and Bax couldn't watch as the man turned over.

Once the guy was facedown, Bax moved in a little, not willing to accidentally see anything that would burn his retinas. He looked at Larry, who had already gone to work on Weinberg's back. The therapist had a look of such disgust on his face that Bax got a chill.

He'd seen that look before, and it was usually immediately followed by someone getting shot. Larry was not happy.

Why in hell didn't Weinberg have a sheet on him? For that matter, why wasn't this massage being done in his suite? According to the brochure, most everything could be done in the guest rooms.

After an unfortunate glimpse of Weinberg's large white ass, Bax turned, ready to end this now. On a credenza, along with bottles and towels, there were three items of interest. A water bottle, a locker key on a bungee cord and a small tape recorder. No, wait. It was a camera. Bax recognized the small device as one he'd seen in the Vice department's bag of tricks. Even from halfway across the room, Bax could see that the recorder was on. The red button glowed in the dark.

He turned back. "I'll let you finish your business here, Mr. Weinberg. We'll speak again."

"I look forward to it, Detective."

As Bax walked toward the door, he looked one last time at Larry. The disgust was gone. In its place, raw fear.

8

IT WAS ALMOST FIVE, and Mia, despite expecting every phone call to be Piper telling her she was fired, kept checking the elevator, waiting for Bax. It was possible, of course, that he'd left the hotel, but he wouldn't do that, would he? Leave without saying anything?

Of course he would. She wasn't his priority. She wasn't even in the top ten. The man was investigating a murder, not obsessing about her. At least not the way she was obsessing about him.

Her private phone rang. "Mia."

"It's me. I found out about Mexico."

"Carlane, that's great."

"One of the first films Weinberg produced was shot in Mexico. It was Bobbi Tamony's first picture, too. Danny Austen was in it, and it was directed by Peter Eccles."

"The whole gang, huh?"

"And, guess what?"

"What?"

"Gerry Geiger was the photographer. He wasn't a pap back then. He worked for Weinberg Films taking publicity stills."

"No."

"Yep. Something happened to shut down shooting for awhile, but I couldn't find out what."

"Really."

"It could have been anything. Weather, permits. It was shot on a shoestring, so who knows. Anyway, the movie did well for the company, and Weinberg was off and running. He used the same team in three other pictures. Eccles, Bobbi and Danny."

"How cozy."

"I'll say. And for what it's worth, the Mexico shoot was the last one Geiger did as an employee. He went freelance after that."

"Okay. Great. I appreciate it so much."

"You can repay me by taking me to lunch with Danny Austen."

Mia winced. "I'll see what I can do."

As soon as she hung up, she printed out her daily log. It was the last thing she had to do before Ellen, the second-shift concierge, took over.

The afternoon had been brutal, one call after another, and while most everything had been taken care of, there were still two items for follow-up. One was a pair of tickets to a sold-out show, the other the limo service for Ms. Tamony, who was going out again tonight, but she hadn't known what time.

Mia waited the few seconds for the printout, then put the page in the book. That was it, she was done. She could go now, get changed, make it to the subway in plenty of time to catch the train. But she didn't leave, not even when Ellen took her place behind the desk.

Mia thought about what Carlane had told her, wondering how Mexico fit into the picture, if it did at all. Then she thought about Weinberg's digital picture collection, and she felt sick to her stomach all over again.

Of course, that made her think about Bax. She knew she

had to tell him that she'd been snooping, and she also knew he wasn't going to be thrilled about that, but she hoped the data she'd gathered would make up for it.

Mia lingered for a few more minutes, looking from the front entrance to the elevator, and then it hit her. She was behaving like a child. A lovesick child. How often had she been scornful of other women for their foolishness around men. She'd been completely intolerant of their constant preoccupation. No man, she'd been certain, would ever turn her into one of those desperate, pathetic creatures.

And here she was.

Breaking and entering. Snooping. Prying. All because she wanted to impress him.

She couldn't kid herself about it any longer. She wanted to solve this murder so that they could be together, yes, but also because she thought he'd like her more if she cracked the case.

Brilliant.

The awful thing was, she barely knew this man. It didn't feel that way. In fact, she could hardly believe they hadn't been close for years, but the truth was they were practically strangers. Even if there was a possibility of something happening between them, her behavior was completely ridiculous.

She'd read enough to know that the human body will go to great lengths to compel the species to replicate. It was biological and therefore unavoidable. And she'd heard of love at first sight, which she'd always enjoyed as a fictional premise, but never thought would happen to her. Even so, the degree of idiocy one exhibits in this particular situation was entirely dependent on character. On willpower, damn it.

With newfound determination to just get on with her life, she resolved to find Bax, tell him what she'd done today, help him with his tabloid questions and then go the heck home. She'd stop at the market to pick up some dinner. Watch some TV. Go to bed. She could use the sleep.

Everything about her reaction to Bax had been wrong. So what that there was a physical spark. He wasn't the only man nor the last man she'd ever feel this way about. The reason it felt remarkable was that it hadn't happened to her before. Not like this. Not as if she'd been hit by a ten-ton truck.

The elevator door opened. A guest walked out.

Then Bax. And yep, there was that big old truck once more, hitting her square in the heart.

"Hey, I was hoping you hadn't left yet."

Mia ignored her body's reaction. After all, biology was not destiny.

"You have plans? I was hoping I could take you to dinner."

"Well…"

"I want to talk to you about those tabloid stories, but mostly about Oscar Weinberg. You think you could spare me a couple of hours?"

She smiled on the outside but inside she was far too aware that she was about to fold like a paper bag. "Sure. Let me go get changed. I'll meet you at the pony wall in the garage."

He shook his head apologetically. "Shit, I'm not quite ready. Can you give me a half hour?"

"Of course."

He walked back into the elevator with her, his hand on the small of her back. Not that it meant anything. Just because her heart pounded and her stomach trembled didn't mean he was touching her in *that way*. She was the informant. He was the cop. Period. End of story.

They parted ways in the basement, with their plans set.

If only she hadn't argued so hard to work with him on this case. Once again, her big mouth had gotten her into trouble, only this time it was a lot more than a job that was at stake.

There was no way to pull out now. She'd crossed the line. Done things she wasn't proud of. Seen things she shouldn't have seen.

She'd been so excited to solve the puzzle. Some puzzle.

Mia changed into jeans and a light sweater, putting her uniform in her tote. She had another in the locker and since tomorrow was her day off, she could get this one to the dry cleaners.

By the time she'd switched shoes, brushed her teeth and checked her makeup, she still had twenty minutes until their meeting.

With a great many misgivings, but knowing she needed to do something, she returned to the garage. Better to step up to the plate, to face Danny Austen and apologize for entering his trailer. If he wanted her gone, so be it.

She knocked on his trailer door, but she got no answer. This time, she knew enough not to just walk inside. Far too relieved, she went down the steps and toward that empty trailer Bax had taken her to. It wasn't empty today.

Nan Collins, she of tabloid fame, was inside, sipping a drink.

"Ms. Collins?"

Nan looked at her. "Yes?"

"I don't know if you remember me. Mia Traverse. I'm the hotel concierge."

"Oh, right. Sure. How you doing?"

"I'm fine. I just wanted to mention I was there the other day when you were doing that scene with Danny. You were awesome."

Nan's whole demeanor changed. She fairly beamed. "You think so?"

Mia took the first step leading inside, but only the first one. "Seriously. I couldn't believe how good you were. I barely noticed Danny at all, and I'm a big fan."

Nan put down her drink. "Come on in. There's soda in the fridge. And rum in the bar."

"Oh, that sounds great." Mia entered the trailer and looked around wide-eyed. "This is pretty fabulous."

"Not nearly as nice as Danny's but it'll do. Make yourself at home."

"Thanks." Mia got a diet soda from the fridge, but passed on the rum. "I know I've seen you in some other pictures. That one where Bobbi played the hooker?"

"I played the high school teacher."

"Too bad it wasn't a bigger part." As Mia sipped her soda, an idea flashed. A crazy one, but hey, what the heck. "Oh, and I remember that one, it was from awhile ago. It was shot in Mexico? What was that one called?"

In a heartbeat, Nan went from welcoming hostess to ice queen. "That wasn't a very good film. I'm surprised you even saw it."

"Oh, no I remember you in it. You were good."

"I barely had one line."

Mia grinned and shrugged. "You've been working on Weinberg films for a long time, though, huh?"

"Listen, Mia, I'm sorry. I forgot. I've got someone coming by in just a couple of minutes, so I'll have to say goodbye. Thanks for stopping in, though."

"No problem. I really enjoyed watching you work."

"Yeah. That's great. Thanks."

Mia barely crossed the threshold before the door was shut in her face. "Bingo," she whispered. Mexico meant something. Hell, it all meant something. But what?

SINCE MAXWELL'S WAS still in use by the film company, she and Bax went to Puttanesca instead. It was a nice Italian place on East 59th with brick walls and cozy tables.

She ordered a watermelon martini just after they sat, which seemed to surprise him. He ordered a glass of merlot.

"So you had questions about the tabloids?"

He sat back. "Maybe this wasn't such a good idea. You're probably beat after the day you've had, and here I am dragging you out. We can get our drinks, maybe an appetizer. Then I'll take you home."

"No, no. It's fine. I am a little tired, but it's okay. We can have dinner."

"You sure?"

"Yeah."

"Okay. Now how about that appetizer?"

She'd been to the restaurant often and from the way he ordered his carpaccio di manzo without a glance at the menu, so had Bax. She ended up with a pear salad to be followed by vodka ravioli. His main course was the gnocchi, which, she knew, was wonderful.

After the waiter left, she sipped her martini and waited for him to talk. Not that she wasn't going to do some talking of her own, she just hadn't figure out exactly how to tell him.

He'd brought a couple of tabloids with him, the two with the largest circulation. "First, I'd like to know if you can identify where these pictures were taken." He unrolled *The National Tattler,* the one with Bobbi Tamony on the cover.

Mia pulled the magazine over and studied not the woman but the background. It didn't take her long to identify the club. "That's Osso."

"Where is that?"

"Upper East Side. Very trendy, hard to get in. From what I can see, this is the back room. You really have to be somebody to get in there."

"What else can you tell me?"

"That's Nan Collins." She pointed to the redhead standing behind Bobbi.

"You know about her?"

"She's with the movie. I've seen her in Weinberg's entourage as well as on the set. She's done a number of films with them."

"Really." Bax put the other magazine out. "Is this Osso?"

Mia sipped her martini then put it down so she could focus. This picture wasn't as clear. There was Danny Austen, and of course she recognized the starlet, but the décor… "No, that's not. It's…damn, what's the name, it's Route 9. It's about five blocks from Osso."

"What else?"

"Nan, again." Mia put the tabloids side by side. "She's wearing the same thing. This was the same night."

"How can you be sure?"

"She has the same kink in her hair." She turned the magazines around and pointed. "That's not on purpose, and I noticed it in the other photo. It's the same night."

She looked up at Bax to find him grinning. Really grinning. She hoped he would still be smiling after she told him about her escapades. "Speaking of Nan," she said.

"Yeah?"

"Well, okay. See, remember that night when the paparazzi attacked us after dinner? One of them, I have no idea which one, said something to me about Mexico. I thought I'd heard him wrong, but then when Sheila Geiger came for that lunch with Piper, she said something about Mexico, too. That I should check on Mexico. Well, that was twice Mexico came up and, well…"

"Mia?"

"I called my friend, Carlane. She knows more about movie stuff than anyone I know. Anyway, she found out that Oscar Weinberg had made a film in Mexico six years ago."

Bax's eyes widened as she filled him in on the rest of what Carlane had told him.

She paused for another sip of the martini before she went on. "So, while I was waiting for you a little while ago, I just happened to walk by that empty motor home, only it was occupied. By Nan Collins."

"And?" he asked.

"We spoke. I mentioned Mexico. She got upset. Visibly upset. Two seconds later, she kicked me out."

"I talked to her, you know," he said. "Nan. She acted as if she was someone important, and I just thought it was her ego, but now I'm thinking she might be."

"Important?"

"Connected. You've seen her with Weinberg."

"Several times. I thought she was sleeping with him."

The look on Bax's face made her laugh.

"I talked to Oscar this afternoon," he said, and it was her turn to be surprised.

"Really?" How close had she come to being caught

red-handed? "He must have come in through the garage because I didn't know he was back."

"He was in the spa getting a massage. Which, just so you know, is not a spectator sport."

"Ew."

"My thoughts exactly. Something was going on with him and the massage therapist. It was a power play, but I'm not at all sure what it meant."

"Who was it?"

"Larry."

Larry Kent. She'd seen a memory card with the initials LK. "Oh. He's been with the spa for a long time. Never heard one bad thing about him."

"It seemed weird to me that Oscar didn't have the massage in his suite."

"He usually does."

"So why not today?"

She thought about it as the waiter brought their appetizers. The salad was heaven, as usual, and man, was she starved. Being a criminal really stirred up the appetite. But she couldn't put this off any longer. "Coincidentally," she began, feeling her face flush, "I happened to be in Oscar Weinberg's suite this afternoon."

"Seems like you've had a busy day."

"Yeah."

"Want to tell me about it?"

She took a deep breath and gave it up. All of it. Halfway through her tale she knew her adventures didn't amuse him and by the time she'd told him everything he was clearly pissed.

He leaned over the table. "Goddamn it, Mia, what the hell were you thinking?"

"I wanted to help."

"By breaking into a guest's room? Aside from the legal issues, of which there are many, what if you'd been caught?"

"I know. It was stupid of me."

"Stupid?" He opened his mouth, then shut it again. After a long, painful moment, he shook his head and said, softly, "It's my fault."

"How is it your fault?"

"I had no business roping you into this mess."

"No. I wanted to help. And I have been a help."

"Yes, you have. But that's over. No more. I appreciate what you've done, but Mia, this was too much. I can't have you taking these chances."

"Okay," she said, "I realize I went too far today, but come on, Bax. I still have more connections than anyone at the hotel."

"I'll find another way."

"How?"

"I don't know. But you're out, Mia. That's final. Someone was murdered. The killer is still on the loose. I'm not going to let you get in the line of fire."

"Now you're just being melodramatic. I might get fired, but I won't get killed."

"Really? You know what I saw when I was in that massage room with Oscar? He was videotaping his session. I saw the camera myself."

"Oh."

"Oh," he repeated. "What makes you think he didn't have another camera in his suite? Maybe one in that closet? One that was triggered to go off if anyone tampered with his mirror?"

The blood rushed from Mia's head and made her momentarily dizzy. It had never occurred to her that she could have been taped. "Damn," she whispered.

"Damn, indeed. I think you should take some time off from work."

"I can't. I just can't."

"Mia, this is getting dangerous."

She shook her head, hardly believing that she'd been such a fool. "But still, now that you know he has those memory cards, can't you get a search warrant?"

"In order to do that, I'd have to take you down to the precinct. And you'd have to admit that you were in the suite illegally. There would be no option but to arrest you, Mia, and once that happened…"

"I'd lose my job."

"It would be a matter of public record. I don't see how you could work as a concierge again."

She got very, very still. This was so much worse than she'd ever imagined. She'd put Bax in a hideous position and herself in the deepest hot water she could imagine. "But you have to," she said.

"I don't have to do anything."

"And if what I saw can solve the murder?"

He sat back in his chair, his unflappable face not so unreadable now. He was worried, terribly so. And angry. Of course, she couldn't blame him. She'd screwed up about as badly as a person could.

"I have to think about this. But first, is there anything else you need to tell me?"

She nodded, and he let out a little groan. She signaled the waiter, needing another drink badly. Then she told him about her trip into Danny Austen's trailer.

By the time the pasta arrived, she had completely lost her appetite. She'd messed up. With the case. With the hotel. With Bax.

Shit.

BAX STOOD IN THE HALLWAY in front of Mia's door. He hated the way he'd left things with her, but what choice was there? If something happened to her...

Goddamn these movie people.

This whole case felt like a can of worms. Every new piece of information made things muddier instead of clearer. He had the feeling it was all there, just out of reach. None of these people were innocent, but which one had wielded the knife that had killed Geiger?

He had to find out about Mexico. Make sure Danny Austen didn't go off the deep end now that Mia had caught him with his pants down. And, he had to figure out some way to get his hands on those memory cards. All before one of them, or all of them, decided that Mia had seen too much.

Shit.

HENRY TOTH ORDERED a full breakfast, complete with juice and coffee. Bax didn't say a word. He needed Toth to clear some things up for him, and if he had to pay for the meal, so be it.

"I don't know that I can be of any more help, Detective. I pretty much told you everything I know the last time we spoke."

"Tell me about Oscar Weinberg."

"That's a pretty broad question."

Bax sat back in the booth in the small diner. They were

several blocks from the hotel, away from the other paparazzi. "I'm in no rush."

Toth shook his head. He still looked as if he hadn't showered, but Bax was starting to understand his unkempt look was all part of a persona he worked hard to maintain. In his conversations with the reporters from Page Six and the other tabloids, it seemed that Toth was one of the powerhouses of street photography. While Geiger had had pretty specific targets, those connected with Oscar Weinberg, Toth didn't seem to care who he shot. Any celebrity in New York was fair game. But he, like most other paps, was never able to get the inside scoop on Gerry's favorite subjects.

"What arrangement did Weinberg have with Geiger? Why was he the one to get the calls?"

"That started a long time ago," Toth said. "From what I hear, Geiger used to work for a film distributor, I forget which one. He was a set photographer. Movie stills, production photos, that kind of thing."

"What happened?"

Toth shrugged. "He went private about six years ago."

"Why?"

"I assume he thought he could make more money on his own."

"What do you know about a film he worked on in Mexico? About six years ago?"

"Nothing. I wasn't doing this shit back then."

"You and Geiger were pretty competitive."

"Yeah. And to tell you the truth, I'm not all that upset that he's dead. But I don't know who killed him."

"What about Oscar?"

"Oscar is a very nervous fellow. And he's good with audio-visual equipment."

"What does he want?"

"Control."

The meal arrived and Toth spent several minutes preparing his feast to his liking. Bax sipped his coffee.

"You know," Henry said, finally. "If it were me, I'd be kind of curious as to why Nan Collins turned down a role as a regular in one of those *Law and Order* series. Seems to me, a gal as ambitious as Nan would have been all over that part. It sure beats the hell out of fetching and toting for Weinberg."

Bax thought about that as Toth ate. In the end, he didn't mind paying for breakfast.

IT WAS TEN IN THE MORNING, and Mia had to get to the dry cleaners. She didn't want to go. She'd had a horrible night. She'd cried until she had no more tears. Burned with shame. Ached as if her heart had been yanked right out of her chest. How could she mourn the loss of something she'd never had? How could it hurt so much when they hadn't even kissed?

He'd been so upset. So angry.

If there had ever been a chance that the two of them might get together, she'd squashed it with her stupidity. With her carelessness.

Inevitably, horribly, there was only one thing that could start to make up for what she'd done. She would quit.

It made her so sad she could barely breathe, but really what choice did she have?

It was going to be awful, explaining to Piper why she had to leave. Confessing. Mia would have to make sure they could cover for her absence because the last thing she wanted to do was leave everyone in the lurch.

But the worst of it was going to be walking away from Hush. Walking away from her dreams. She wouldn't even ask for a letter of recommendation or a reference. She didn't deserve either.

The film company was shooting on the corner, and she had to wait until they let traffic go to cross into the garage. She passed the trailers, keeping her head low, not out of fear but embarrassment.

When she stepped into the hotel, the urge was strong to turn around and run, but she kept going. She had no choice. But now she had to let Bax know she was here. God forbid he should see her, and think she was up to something.

She stopped in the hallway and got out her cell. In a fit of optimism, she'd put his number into speed dial. It rang four times, then his voice mail came on. Just hearing him brought tears to her eyes.

"Hi. It's Mia. I'm at the hotel, but don't worry, I won't be here long. I've come to turn in my resignation. I'm going to see if Piper's available. If she's not, then I'll leave her a note. I'll explain what I did, and we'll have it on record so you won't get in trouble."

She had to pause as her throat closed, but when she could talk again there was only one thing left to say. "I'm sorry."

She hung up and headed for the concierge desk.

Tina was working this morning. She was nice and she was good. She or Ellen would probably be moved to Mia's hours. God, even thinking that hurt.

"Is Piper here?"

"Yeah, she is, but she had a meeting with Sheila Geiger that started about an hour ago. I think it's still going on."

Mia nodded, wondering if she should wait, or write out her resignation. It wouldn't hurt to do both. "I just need to get some paper," she said, taking out a few sheets of Hush stationery.

"No sweat. It was really busy this morning, but thankfully things have settled way down."

"That's great," she said. "Listen, I'm going to be in the cafeteria. Could you give me a call if you see Piper's finished with her meeting?"

"Sure."

Mia walked as if to the gallows. Everything in her body ached, especially her heart. Writing this letter was going to kill her, she felt sure of that.

She found herself an empty table and she began. She wrote slowly and carefully, not leaving out a thing. Bax was not going to get screwed over this. She and she alone was responsible.

By the time she'd put it all on paper, it was almost noon. She'd gone through a half-dozen tissues and several sheets of paper. But it was done.

God, how was she going to tell her parents?

She went to the trash and tossed her tissues and then her phone rang. It wasn't Bax. In fact, it was a number she didn't recognize. Probably a solicitation. "Hello?"

"Miss Traverse?" It was a woman's voice, high, with a distinct Brooklyn accent.

"Yes."

"Detective Milligan asked me to call. He's having trouble with his phone. He'd like you to meet him in the garage, by the north exit."

"Oh, okay. Thank you." Mia hung up. For a second she allowed herself to believe things would be okay, at least with Bax. But the truth was too heavy to dismiss.

She would show him her letter to Piper, see if he wanted anything changed. Then she would say goodbye.

The walk to the north exit took a while, not because it

was all that far, but because her feet didn't want to move. She willed herself to stop crying. She had all the time in the world to do that after she was home.

Bax wasn't there, at least as far as she could see. "Bax? Hello?"

No answer. Odd. She would have called him if his phone had been working.

Instead, she rounded one of the big movie trucks that had been parked there all week. She had a pretty good field of vision then, but still no sight of Bax. "Hello?"

Her phone rang, making her jump, and as she reached for it, the top of her shoulder exploded in pain and she tripped, fell, smashed into the pavement.

"Ride of the Valkyries" played as everything went dark.

9

"MIA, WHERE ARE YOU? Call me back." Bax was in the garage after his meeting with Henry Toth. The concierge on duty had told him she thought Mia had gone out to the trailers, which made him angry all over again. Hadn't she heard him last night? Hadn't she told him she wouldn't come back to the hotel?

He walked to the middle half block of the long parking area. It felt empty, at least of people if not vehicles. Goddamn it, why wasn't she picking up? He was going to read her the riot act the second he found her.

He hit her speed dial number again. Could she have gone to the trailers? Looking for him, perhaps? She wouldn't be crazy enough to approach Nan again or Danny. Or would she? Her phone rang once, twice, three times, and that was it, he'd had it with—wait. He pulled the phone from his ear. There. "Ride of the Valkyries." Small, distant, faint.

It stopped, and he dialed again, hurrying toward the sound. As the tune got louder, he pulled his weapon from the holster. This was not good. The garage was dark on this side, with mostly empty trucks stacked one after another. To the best of his knowledge there wasn't a full-time security guard over here, as there was nothing much to see. The guards concentrated their efforts on primary targets, the hotel entrances, the motor homes and the production trailers.

He called again, more grateful than ever for speed dial. Wagner's music was louder now, echoing. Right behind that truck.

He put his phone away, put both hands on his weapon as he crouched low and hurried around the truck. His heart fell as he saw her on the ground. There was way too much blood.

Barely aware of how he'd gotten there, he crouched by her side, feeling her neck for a pulse. She was, thank God, still alive.

Bax pulled out his phone and called for a bus, and then he called the concierge desk of Hush. He told the blond girl to call the set nurse and send him to the north exit in the garage.

Then he was all about making sure Mia didn't die.

He found the wound. It didn't look too bad. Just the top of her shoulder. But, oh, shit, she was bleeding from a gash on her temple.

He wasn't sure if he should try to stem the bleeding or leave her for the EMTs in case she'd hurt her neck.

She moaned and then her eyes opened and Bax was so relieved he could barely breathe.

"Bax?"

"Shh, honey. Just rest. You're gonna be fine."

"What happened?"

Thankfully, the set nurse came running and a few seconds later he'd pushed Bax out of the way to take over.

All Bax could do was watch and wait for the ambulance. He could still hardly believe that some sonofabitch had shot her. Tried to kill her. The thought of it, the idea that she— He wanted to hit someone. Pummel the prick. Everything in him screamed for vengeance.

One thing for goddamn sure. Whoever did this would pay if it was the last thing Bax did.

The nurse, a guy in his early thirties with a meticulous beard, looked to Bax as if he knew what he was doing. He also ignored the shoulder wound, concentrating on Mia's head. After cleaning and bandaging her temple, he probed her scalp, her neck. Then asked her, "Can you tell me your name, sweetie?"

"Mia Traverse."

"Do you know where you are?"

"Hush?"

Bax paced the area around the truck as he called the precinct to get some CSI out here. He looked for the ambulance, then back at Mia. After he'd arranged for a detective to get out here, he spoke to Miguel, still on desk duty but helpful nonetheless. It didn't take long to give him the details of what Bax needed, and then the bus arrived. Soon, Mia was on a stretcher and hooked up to a heart monitor.

A crowd had formed, mostly movie people, and as Bax climbed into the back of the ambulance he saw Danny Austen standing right next to Nan Collins. Anger swept through him like a tornado, but he held himself back. Mia came first.

Making sure he wasn't in the way, he watched the EMTs work on her. She was still a little dopey, but she hadn't exhibited signs of a severe concussion. That didn't mean he'd rest until they did a full exam and CT scan. He was just grateful her color was good and so was her heart.

As they neared the hospital, Bax moved down the bench a bit so Mia could see him. He smiled at her, and she smiled back. He couldn't believe how scared he'd been. How deeply he cared that she was all right.

He hardly knew this woman, but damn it, there was nothing in his world that was more important than keeping her safe.

"Ride of the Valkyries" made him jump, then pat his pockets. It was her phone. When had he grabbed it? He looked at the caller ID. Piper Devon. No way he was giving the phone to Mia, and personally, he wasn't ready for this call, not yet.

Mia came first.

BAX. SHE OPENED her eyes, and he was right there. Right next to her. It was tempting to try to touch the hand resting on her arm, but moving hurt her head. A lot.

"Hey, beautiful. You're up."

"What's—" Her mouth was dry as the desert and her tongue felt too big.

Bax brought a plastic spoon to her lips. "Open," he said. "Ice."

She obeyed and the cold wet felt wonderful. "What's going on?"

"You're in the hospital. You fell."

"Oh."

"And you were shot."

She swallowed her ice. "What?"

"It's okay. You aren't hurt badly. The bullet just grazed your shoulder. You had eight stitches. And four where you hit your head. Don't worry, though. The doctor said your concussion is minor and the worst of it's going to be a headache."

"I was shot?"

He nodded. "Why in hell were you back at the hotel?"

She blinked at him for a few seconds, then sighed. "I went there to resign."

Bax touched the side of her face with his fingertips. "You should have talked to me, kiddo."

"I tried. Honest." Tears came, sudden and hot. "I'm so sorry."

He covered her hand with his. "Shh. It's okay. As long as you're all right, I don't give a damn about another thing."

"I was just so stupid."

"Yeah, you were. It happens. We move on."

"Now you're just being nice."

He grinned at her. "Yeah. I am."

She would have socked him if she could have. "Where was I shot?"

"It was more of a graze than a shot—"

"No, I mean where."

"Oh. The garage. You don't remember?"

"I remember writing my resignation. Waiting to talk to Piper."

"The doctor said you might have some amnesia around the incident. It doesn't matter. You're going to be fine. I promise. And I'm going to find out who did this to you. Trust me."

She squeezed his fingers. "I do. With my life."

"I think that's the medicine talking." He gave her another spoon of ice. "It's late. You should go back to sleep."

"What about you?"

"Don't worry about me. I'll be right here when you get up." He brushed her forehead gently. "Right here."

Knowing he would be, she slept.

BAX WAS ON HIS SECOND cup of coffee when she woke up. It was early, not yet seven, but she'd had a good night. From what the nurse said, she was strong. It should be a quick recovery.

It couldn't happen fast enough for him. When he thought about her lying in that pool of blood, it made him sick to his stomach. All through the long afternoon and night, he'd beaten himself up for bringing her into such danger. He'd been such an idiot. He should have realized she was too curious to let things be. That she was so into solving the case that she'd let her good judgment slip. When it came right down to it, he'd have willingly let the killer go free if it meant keeping Mia from harm.

He'd been so scared. Like nothing he could remember.

"Hi," she said.

"Hi."

"I'm still in the hospital."

"Yep." He'd been getting fresh ice all night, in case she woke up. He'd filled the cup only a half hour ago. Giving her a spoonful, he marveled again at how small she was. The lengths he would go to to keep her safe.

"What time is it?"

"Almost seven."

"AM or PM?"

"Morning. You slept through the night."

"Did you get any rest?"

"Enough."

"Liar."

"Hey."

She smiled at him. That alone made the uncomfortable night worth it.

"I want to sit up."

"Tell you what. You let me get the nurse in here, then we'll see."

"Okay," she said. "Whatever you say."

Bax was thrown out of the room as the nurse attended to Mia. He couldn't make phone calls in the hallway so he went to the waiting room. He called Piper. They'd spoken last night, and he'd promised her word first thing. Then he called Grunwald.

The CSI guys had combed the whole damn garage, but they hadn't found the bullet or a casing. So they had nothing. No one seemed to know why Mia had been in that part of the garage, and the doctor had said she might never remember.

His gut told him it was Oscar Weinberg who ordered the hit. He didn't believe that oaf would do the shooting himself, but damn it, she'd gotten too close when she found those memory cards.

By this time, Weinberg had probably ditched them. Even if Bax could get a search warrant, he was damn sure he'd come up empty.

Not that he could afford to eliminate Danny Austen or Nan Collins from his list of suspects, but neither of them seemed as likely as Oscar.

Bax wanted to go straight to the hotel and put a bullet through the fat fuck's head, but he wouldn't. He'd follow the rules because that's what he did. But there wasn't going to be a thing he didn't know about Weinberg. Not one thing. And he would be there to watch as they led him to prison.

"Detective?"

It was the nurse.

"How is she?"

"Remarkably well. Rounds have already started, so the doctor will be in soon. But I can't see why she'd need to stay here. She'll have to take it easy, and you'll have to watch her for the next few days, but she should be able to go home."

"Are you sure? If there's any risk—"

"The doctor will fill you in on what to look for."

"Thanks," he said, wondering how in hell he was going to take care of her and solve the damn case at the same time. He'd figure something out.

Before he went back to her room, he got another cup of ice and yet another coffee. Mia smiled at him, and she looked so good sitting up that several of the knots in his neck released their hold. The only evidence that she'd been hurt was a goose egg that was thankfully much reduced from the night before. There was a bandage on her shoulder, of course, but she looked great. Beautiful. Alive.

Just then, the doctor came, trailed by his posse of medical students, their white coats and stethoscopes bright in the light from the window.

He went into the hall again, wishing he'd brought his coffee. Leaning against the pale-blue wall he thought about what to do with her. He didn't want her to go to her apartment. Going to his apartment didn't make much sense, either. Maybe she could stay with one of her friends. He didn't think her parents were in New York, but if all else failed, he'd ship her to them.

He checked his watch three times before the doctors left, and craned to hear what he could. Turns out he needn't have bothered as the doctor et al called him in and explained everything he'd need to know. What to look for, when to give her the antibiotics, all of it. He'd given Mia a prescription for pain pills, too, but he didn't think she'd need them past today. Finally, they were alone again.

"I get to go home."

He nodded as he sat. "We need to talk about that."

"What do you mean?"

"I don't want you to be alone," he said.

The light in her eyes faded a bit. "Someone really tried to kill me."

"I'm going to find out who."

"I just—" She stopped, her gaze on the door.

He turned to see Piper Devon carrying a Barneys bag. She was a stunning woman, one who commanded attention even when stock still and silent. She had that rarefied air about her, the kind that comes with a lifetime of money and breeding.

"May I come in?"

Bax stood, pulled the chair back a bit and waited for Mia's boss to sit down.

"I brought you some things," Piper said. "I figured you wouldn't have much to wear." She held up the bag. "It should do for today."

Mia's cheer had disappeared and her eyes gleamed with unshed tears. "I'm so sorry."

"You didn't shoot yourself," Piper said kindly.

"There are things you don't know."

Ms. Devon sighed. "You mean about you going into Mr. Weinberg's suite? About your resignation?"

"How did you—"

"You dropped your letter in the garage. I have to say, going into the suite wasn't your most shining moment. But no, I'm not going to accept your resignation."

Mia looked from Piper to Bax and back again. The tears that had threatened glided down her soft cheeks. "I don't understand."

"I know you were trying to help, and more than that, I know you won't do anything remotely like that again, yes?"

"Never."

"Then it's settled." Piper turned to Bax. "I'm going to put her up at the hotel, Detective. I've arranged to have her guarded until you find out who did this to her."

"That's great," Bax said. "I can keep my eye on her, too."

"I assumed," Piper said, then she turned back to Mia. "You're going to stay in that room until there's no more danger, right? No more trying to solve mysteries, no more walking in on actors unannounced?"

"Yes, ma'am."

"Good. Since you're being released, why don't you get dressed and we'll get you to the hotel. I've got the limo downstairs." Piper left the bag on the bed, then went into the hall.

"Oh, Bax," Mia whispered. "I can't believe it."

"You're lucky," he said. "In so many ways."

She sniffed, and wiped her cheeks with her hands, wincing as she lifted her left arm.

"Do you need help getting dressed?"

"No, I'm fine."

"Yell when you're ready," he said.

Piper met him in the hallway, and for the next twenty minutes he ran down every lead, every rumor and every possibility. Then, after telling him that her decision not to fire Mia had more to do with the hotel's reputation than being a nice person, she asked him if he could catch the bad guy.

"I will," he said. "Count on it."

10

THE PILLS, AND MIA COULDN'T remember the name of them, worked really, really well. Or maybe her pain had been lifted out of the sheer joy she felt that she wasn't fired.

Probably the pills, though.

The limo ride back to Hush was sweet and quiet. Quiet because she was afraid of saying something stupid. Sweet because Bax held her hand the whole way.

The dress Piper had brought her fit like a dream and didn't even need to be hemmed. It occurred to her that perhaps it had been purchased from the kid's department. Didn't matter. It was simple and easy to wear and she thanked God she'd shaved her legs this morning. Uh, yesterday morning. Yesterday, before she'd been shot.

It still felt so odd. Her. Shot. With a gun. Someone wanted her dead, and now she was moving into a room at the hotel to be safe.

Surreal didn't even begin to describe it.

They reached the hotel and from what Mia could see, there was no filming going on. At least not outside. Perhaps they were inside, in Exhibit A. Or a location away from the hotel. She doubted they had called things off because of the shooting.

Piper accompanied them to the front desk. Mia could

tell everyone wanted to ask her questions, find out how she was, but nobody spoke because, well, of Piper. She picked up the key they had ready, then turned to Bax. "Take Mia up. There's everything she'll need for awhile. I suggest you get some rest yourself. You look like hell."

"Thanks. For everything."

"Find this bastard," she said. "Put him away forever."

"Yes, ma'am."

Piper gave Mia a pointed look. "Don't do anything dumb." Then she left, heading back toward the front entrance.

"That was very cool." Mia thought about taking Bax's hand again, but didn't.

"Let's go." He walked her to the elevator, then pressed the button for the 14th floor.

"What's the room number?"

"1406."

"That's not a room. That's a suite."

"Really?"

Mia nodded, but that pulled on her shoulder and made her head feel weird. "This is unbelievably generous. You know how much those suites go for?"

"Nope."

"Well, I don't remember. But it's oodles and oodles." She turned to him, which wasn't so simple. She had to turn from the waist up. Then, because she liked the sound of it, she said it again. "Oodles. Oodles and oodles. What are you giggling about?"

"I don't giggle."

"Sounded like a giggle to me."

"It was a manly chortle."

"Ha," she said, then faced the elevator door again. "Chortle my behind."

He did it again. A verifiable giggle.

"I'LL SLEEP LATER," Bax said, anxious to get down to his office and talk to Grunwald. A hell of a lot had happened since the shooting, and he felt completely out of the loop. Not that he would have done anything differently, but now was not the time to lie down.

"You have to sleep, even if it's just for a twenty-minute power nap." Mia gave him her puppy-eyed stare. "Please?"

She was in bed, with a bottle of designer water on the night table, along with a small bowl of fresh fruit and the TV remote. Her cell phones were both on the bed next to her. The only thing he hadn't wanted within reach was the bottle of pain pills. They worked, all right, but she was loopy from them. What she needed was rest.

At least here, in the security of the suite with the guard on duty just outside the door, she wouldn't have to be scared. And he could concentrate on the case instead of worrying every minute about her safety.

But damn, the bed looked big and soft and it was tempting as hell. "I'll come back in an hour. That's when you're supposed to have your next antibiotic, anyway. I'll rethink sleep then."

She started to shake her head, then stopped. "I'm going to call you in one hour and annoy you until you climb into this bed. You hear me?"

He did. His gaze shifted to the armoire. It was closed, and he hadn't seen inside it. But he knew what was hiding. What waited. What he was a callous, insensitive bastard for even thinking about.

Which was just another reason for him to get the hell out of here. Away from sex cabinets and loopy women. "Rest. Heal. I'll be back in an hour."

She smiled at him. "I brushed my teeth."

That stopped him. "That's great."

"I mean, before I got into bed. I'm minty fresh now."

He moved a bit closer to her, wondering if he should be worried. "Minty fresh is good."

Her sigh was twice as big as she was. "So if a person, say a person who'd saved another person's life, wanted to kiss a person, it would be okay because that person had brushed her teeth."

"Ah."

"Geez. Talk about slow."

"I don't know, Mia. There's still the case and—"

"We almost lost me yesterday. Do you think it's smart to put this off?"

He opened his mouth, but whatever he was going to say vanished in light of her statement. So he did what he probably should have done when he'd first had the urge. He touched her cheek with his palm then took her in a kiss that made more sense than anything had in years. She was, indeed, minty fresh.

If anyone had accused him of tearing up, he would have denied it to the death, but damn it, he was glad she was here.

When he finally pulled back and looked into her dark eyes, the small remnants of his doubts and reasons became like dust on the wind. He kissed her forehead, glad there was no fever, glad she didn't hurt too badly, and very glad that this was where he'd return to when the workday ended.

"Be careful out there," she whispered. "Someone's playing for keeps."

"You have my word."

BAX LOOKED AT HIS NOTES, worried that if he didn't transcribe them now, he wouldn't be able to read his own writing. But Mia was upstairs needing her medicine. He closed his notebook and left.

The call had been helpful. Very helpful. That, connected with the memory cards Mia had found in Weinberg's suite had helped him paint a picture. A story, he believed, which began in 2001 in Churubusco movie studio in Mexico.

There were still missing pieces, and he still couldn't put the knife that killed Gerry Geiger in the hand of the killer, or say for certain who had shot Mia, but he knew that not many of these movie people were innocent. Murder, blackmail, collusion all leading back to one primary motive—money. Money for private jets and fancy suites and yachts in Cannes and all the other bullshit that made small men feel big.

It was the same motive that kept gangs in business despite the human toll. The same thing that made one guy beat up another guy at a bar.

Mia was finished as his informant, finished as everything but patient until this mess was over. But that didn't mean he couldn't talk things through with her. Get her opinion. She was smart and she understood these particular baddies better than he did. She was around celebrities and high society on a daily basis, while Bax did his best to avoid those kind of folks.

She'd be a good sounding board. Even if the medicine did make her a little nuts.

He was relieved to find the security guard awake and alert by the suite. He'd have to remember to get the guy something to eat, if Piper hadn't already seen to it.

It only took a minute to discover that meals and everything else had been handled by one of Piper's assistants. Good to know.

Bax used his key and entered the suite as quietly as possible. If Mia was sleeping, he wasn't about to wake her.

He hadn't really looked at the room, well rooms, that Piper had so generously given. They were ridiculously elegant with an unbelievable view of Manhattan. The floor was gold and black tile, the couches made of some shimmery material he didn't recognize. Everything was gold, green or black, and while he wouldn't have thought that could work, work it did.

No detail had been left untended. Fresh flowers filled black vases. A fantastic assortment of beverages and snacks filled the large pantry. The TV on the wall was at least fifty-two inches of flat-panel luxury.

But nothing could hold his attention like the woman in the bedroom. He made his way to the door and peeked in. Mia was nestled in a cocoon of pillows, her dark hair messy and sexy against the pure white of the sheets. She wasn't sleeping, but she hadn't seen him yet, which was just fine, at least for now.

It was easy to see that the doctors had done a good job with her. She wasn't feverish or too uncomfortable. On the contrary, she looked relaxed. Dazzling.

He'd thought a lot about what she'd said. They *had* almost lost her. A few inches over and she would have been a goner. Lost forever. And he would have been heart-broken, not just with guilt, but with remorse.

This woman, this slip of a girl, was something special. Something he'd never thought he'd encounter. He might have been a fan of romantic literature, but he'd treated it as fiction. As unlikely to occur in his life as encountering Bigfoot or the Loch Ness Monster.

And there she was. She'd turned his head. Tweaked his heart. He wanted to know everything there was to know about her. Everything she loved or hated. What she tasted like, and how she sounded when she made love.

He would have set about to do just that, if he wasn't so worried about hurting her. She'd been shot less than twenty-four hours ago. He wasn't about to send her to the hospital just because he was horny.

"Are you ever going to come in?" she said.

He should have known. "I was watching you," he said.

"I know. You were also thinking, and that has me worried."

"Not as worried as I am. How do you feel?"

"I'm sore, but I'll live."

"You need a pill?"

She moved her head a bit. "Yeah, I think so. If I don't move I seem to be okay. Although now that I'm thinking about it, it kind of throbs. See what happens when people think?"

"Throbbing occurs?"

"Very funny, Detective."

He got her medicine from the dresser and made sure she had a full bottle of water. Then he hovered as she drank.

"One more thing," she said as she handed him the almost empty bottle.

"Your wish is my command."

"Help me get up. I need to go to the bathroom."

"You should have called me earlier."

"I didn't need to go earlier."

He put her good arm around his shoulder as he helped her to her feet. Once up, she seemed quite capable of handling things. At least that's what he interpreted from the slap she gave his butt.

"It's time for your nap," she said. "When I get back, it's lights out, mister."

"It's only four-thirty."

"Oh. Then order yourself some dinner, then it's bedtime for real."

"You want me to stay?"

Even though she was but a few steps from the bathroom, she stopped, turned completely around and put her hands on her hips, which looked even tinier in her big sleep shirt. "We're not going to have this argument. I need you here. You need to be here. End of story."

"Yes, ma'am."

"Okay. Now I really need to pee."

He smiled as she disappeared behind the door, but his grin faded along with his energy. Just thinking about going to bed made him dizzy with yearning.

Tonight, at least, nothing was going to happen except sleep. Tomorrow things might change, but tonight? Healing took precedence. Rest. And some food wouldn't hurt.

Mia came back, and after settling her down, he dug up the room service menu. It was more like a novel, it had so many pages, although many of those were filled with the extensive wine selections.

"You hungry?" he asked.

"Yeah, but just for soup. They make a fabulous War Wonton. I'll have that."

He ordered them both dinner, not even flinching at the prices, then emptied his pockets in preparation for bed. He didn't, however, take off his shoulder holster. His weapon would be damn close to wherever he was sleeping. Which appeared to be on the left side of the big old bed.

He kicked off his shoes and climbed aboard. She was close, touching distance. But, he reminded himself for the tenth time, not tonight. "You good?"

"I'm good."

"I heard back from my source in Mexico. Well, my partner's source."

"Wow, tell me."

"It seems someone, a local girl who was working on the Weinberg picture, was killed during the filming."

"I kind of figured it had to be a big deal, but I didn't think it would be another murder."

"There's no proof that it was a murder. According to the police from Churubusco, it was an accident. Somehow she got hold of what she thought was a prop gun. Only it had real bullets. She was dead before she hit the ground."

"But if that's what happened, why would Nan be all upset about it?"

"According to my friend, the official story was a lot more about bribes than truth. A murder investigation would have stopped filming, would have cost Weinberg a hell of a lot. He wasn't insured for a murder, not like with this picture."

"Lesson learned, huh?"

"Yeah. I think someone from the company killed that girl, and it wasn't an accident at all. My friend said the hardest part for the Churubusco police was covering up the fact that the girl had ligature marks on her ankles and wrists."

"Oh, God. How does he know this stuff?"

"Miguel's friend is the captain of a major precinct in Mexico City. He was working his way up the food chain back then. He knows a lot of people."

"So who do you think did it? My money's on Oscar. He just creeps me out."

"I'm having a meeting tomorrow with that massage guy, Larry. I want to find out what freaked him out so badly."

"You can't just go get those memory thingies from Weinberg's room? I bet you a zillion dollars there's enough evidence in there to lock him away for a long time."

"And I'd be willing to bet the farm those memory cards are long gone from Weinberg's suite. But that doesn't mean we won't find them. At the moment though, my main person of interest is Nan. Her name just keeps cropping up. I'm going to find out why."

"She's very vain, you know. Desperate for compliments."

"I wonder, do you think she can act?"

"I don't know. She's been at it for awhile and she keeps getting little roles in Weinberg pictures."

"Someone told me she was offered a recurring role on a TV series."

"When?"

"Recently."

"That'll change her life."

"Not really. She turned it down."

Mia turned too quickly in her surprise and she hissed at the pain. "That makes no sense. She's been a bit player for years and she was pathetically grateful when she thought I'd seen her work."

"Exactly. Something is fishy there. Even if she doesn't know everything, I'm willing to bet she knows a lot."

"Go get 'er Bax. Make her sing like a bird. Squeal like a rat."

"Pills?"

Mia sighed. "I hope so."

MIA'S HEAD FELT BETTER, especially now that it was cradled in the nook of Bax's neck. She'd slept after dinner, amazingly comfortable next to him.

He'd called his friend Grunwald—did he have a first name?—who'd brought an overnight case and some clothes. They'd talked in the other room as she'd drifted in and out, but now they were down for the night, Bax in his pale blue pajama bottoms, her in the sleep T Piper had picked up for her.

It was as if they'd done this a hundred times before. Maybe it was the pills, but she doubted it. There was a connection between them, and she was too tired and sore to do anything but be glad for it.

He had the TV on, showing some creature feature, but the sound was down so low she wondered if he could even hear it. The glow in the bedroom was nice, though.

His arm was around her shoulders, and as she'd assured him, he wasn't hurting her at all. His hand with those nice long fingers rested just under her neck.

She was almost glad that they couldn't do more than this. It would be nice to feel better and to get to know his body, feel him inside her, but for now she wanted his comfort. She loved that she could touch his bare chest, with that nice soft smattering of dark hair. That she could feel him breathe and know that he would be there when she woke.

It still made her throat close when she thought about all Piper had done for her. It amazed her, and humbled her, and made her more determined than ever to be the best employee Hush ever had. She would make up for her lapse in judgment, that was a solemn promise.

No matter what happened, she was going to show Piper and Bax that their faith in her wasn't a mistake.

"You okay?" he whispered.

"I'm fine. I thought you were asleep."

"I was. But I'm not used to all this luxury."

"I know, the bed is awesome."

"I meant having you next to me."

She sighed.

"I think you're supposed to have another pill soon."

"I don't need one. I'm fine."

"Are you sure? It's been four hours."

"Honest. My head hardly hurts."

"What about your shoulder."

"If I'm still, it's okay. Don't worry about me. You need to sleep."

He kissed the top of her head. "It has been a long couple of days."

"You didn't introduce me to your partner."

"Yeah, I know."

"Ashamed of me, are you?"

"No. Him. He's a good detective but he's better when he doesn't have to actually speak to people."

She laughed. "Is that why he's never here?"

"Uh-huh. Grunwald likes the detail work. He does the reports, follows up with the lab, tracks down suspects on the computer."

"You don't like that stuff?"

"Nope. I like talking to real people, hearing their voices and watching their body language. I can never learn enough by reading a tax form or a rap sheet."

"No wonder we get along so well," she said. "I love the puzzles. The Internet is my favorite toy. I can find practically anything on there. But I've learned that a single source is never enough. It's the combination of facts, the melding of information. That's what gets the job done."

"It's good that you love what you do. That's a gift."

Her eyes drifted closed as she thought about that.

Bax turned off the TV and she heard the remote meet the night table.

"Do you think you'll find that in Boulder?" she asked.

He didn't answer her, and she let it go, drifting as she was into sleep.

"I used to think so," he said softly after a long while. "But I might have gotten things all wrong."

She told him not to worry. Or maybe she dreamed that part.

11

BAX WOKE UP TO THE FEEL of Mia against his body. The shaky truth of it kept his eyes closed for a long moment as he traced the sensation from his chest to his thigh. How warm she was and how that warmth seeped into him the way syrup sweetens a pancake. He smelled her, too, as if flowers had been sewn in the mattress.

All they'd done was sleep in the same bed. He'd barely touched her lips with his own, tasted only a hint of her, but she'd rested her head on his shoulder. Her bare foot, cool and remarkably smooth, had run over his shin. She'd snuffled a few times, and even snored a bit, but it wasn't a bad sound at all.

Two days ago it had really bothered him that he couldn't ask her out. That there wouldn't be time enough to get to know her before he left for Boulder and his new life.

Waking up to her heat and her scent and the memory of her sleepy whisper in his ear, it felt as if he'd never had a more intimate experience with another person in his life.

He thought, oddly, of Mia's favorite book. How Lizzy Bennet and Mr. Darcy fell so deeply in love with their arguments and wrong turns and their fussy dances. They'd become lovers in the most old-fashioned way. Quaintly. Sweetly. With a kiss, with a confession, against all reason.

He opened his eyes to find Mia scrunched next to him, her short hair spiked, her sleep T bunched up around her waist baring a strip of her pale tummy, and just the sight of that pink flesh made him harder than he'd been in a long, long time.

He wasn't going to do anything about it. Feel the ache, yes. Marvel at how heavy his balls could get when they wanted attention. But she was healing still and the way he felt about her was all out of proportion and just plain nuts.

It was better to close his eyes again. He had no idea what time it was, just that it was early and soon he would have to face the liars and the thieves and the killers when all he wanted was to stay in this bed with Mia for the rest of his life. Room service would deliver, and he'd never turn on the news, not even once.

His thoughts drifted, the ache from his cock his anchor.

The next time his eyes opened, Mia was sitting up, propped by pillows, her hair still spiked, her skin still pale, except for the bruise on her temple. It was purple and looked like it would hurt a lot if touched.

"I wasn't sure if I should wake you," she said.

"What time is it?"

"Almost eight."

"How long have you been sitting there?"

"Since almost seven."

He stretched beneath the blanket, then smiled at her. "I don't suppose you snuck away and ordered coffee."

She started to shake her head, then stopped with a wince. A few seconds went by and she continued to shake her head only much more slowly. "I was too busy watching you sleep."

"Busy? Did I say anything?"

She wrinkled her nose. "No. You didn't even snore."

"And yet—"

"And yet I couldn't take my eyes off you."

He took a deep breath and turned over, not wanting her to see how the words had affected him. "I have to get up," he said, half into the pillow. "How do you feel? You need your antibiotic."

"Better than I expected," she said. "Good enough to call for coffee. What else? Juice? Bagels? Eggs?"

"Onion bagel," he said. "Cream cheese. Coffee. Cream."

"Got it."

They climbed out of the bed at the same time, her to the phone, him to the bathroom. He wasn't sure if he was still hard from before or if this was new. It didn't matter in the end. He'd shower, take care of things, get on with the business of detecting. Make sure whoever had hurt Mia would never hurt anyone again.

He brushed his teeth, shaved, did all the typical morning stuff, but the shower waited until he went back and checked on Mia. "You need to use the john?"

She scurried past him. "Oh, yeah."

While she was occupied, he got his clothes together and he didn't think about her in her sleep shirt, or about that little flash of belly. He thought instead about Nan Collins and Oscar Weinberg and how he was going to proceed. First, he would talk to Oscar, work on his enormous ego. The man thought he was light-years smarter than anyone else, and that was a mistake Bax could use to his advantage.

Nan would be next, and her fear would be her undoing.

But he couldn't eliminate Danny completely, not yet. There was still the business of his secret and how far he would go to keep it.

Then it was his turn to shower and no matter how he struggled to keep his mind on business, he always came back to Mia. First, that when she was better, he wanted to get in here with her, because this was one wild shower. It had a bunch of different showerheads, one he didn't understand at all. In the end, it didn't matter. He was wet, and slick and there was nothing noble about his thoughts. As he stroked himself it wasn't just a flash of her stomach, it was all of her naked and writhing on the pure white sheets. She was perfect and he explored every inch of her body with his hands, his tongue. He came to the thought of making her come, of making her cry out his name. God, it had been forever since he'd wanted like this. No, he never had wanted like this. Since college he'd never had to wait and he wondered if in all the sexual freedom something good had been lost. Anticipation was highly seductive, especially when each encounter with Mia had given him more fuel for his internal fire.

The rest of his shower went quickly, dressing, too. By the time he went back to the bedroom, the coffee had arrived.

She'd ordered herself some scrambled eggs and toast, and they went to the living room to eat.

Mia hadn't changed from her sleep shirt, which made him crazily happy. It was the mixture, he thought, of intimacy and restraint. The surroundings helped, too, as if they were playing very upscale house.

"Did you take your pill?" he asked.

She nodded. Carefully. "Just the antibiotic. I'm feeling pretty darn good, considering."

"Your shoulder?"

"Not bad at all. Whoever shot me wasn't very good at it."

"Small favors."

"Yeah, but it says something, doesn't it? I was pretty much a static target. Someone who knew about guns wouldn't have grazed my shoulder like that."

"You have a point. Although the shot may have been a warning."

"Maybe, but I doubt it. I think whoever did it was trying to get me to stop asking questions, sure, but they were scared. And if I had to guess, I'd say Oscar was behind it all. He would never do something as a gauche as pulling the trigger, but he would certainly have one of his minions do it."

"Which brings us back to Nan."

"Oh?"

"According to several sources, she's pretty much been Weinberg's lapdog since Mexico."

"Why?"

"I'm guessing it's all connected to that girl's death. Combine that with Oscar's penchant for recording everything, along with Gerry Geiger's photography skills, and you've got a pretty convincing case for blackmail."

"But who's blackmailing whom?"

Bax shook his head. "Since Nan is the only one who didn't benefit, it stands to reason she's being blackmailed."

"And Gerry Geiger was the one who got all the tips. So maybe Oscar and Gerry were in cahoots." Mia sipped some coffee, then laughed.

"What?"

"Cahoots."

"Ah."

"But seriously, this is all making a lot of sense."

"Now if only there was a way to prove any of it."

"Oh, that."

He went to work on his bagel and she did the same with her eggs. The view out the window made him like New York all over again, but the view inside kicked Manhattan's ass.

"Why are you grinning like a loon?" she asked. "Not that you're not adorable, but…"

"A loon, huh?"

"Not the bird, you understand."

"Yeah, I figured."

"Well?"

"Just extremely glad you weren't—"

"Killed?"

He nodded.

"Me, too." She was sitting on one of the green chairs while he had landed on the couch, the breakfast setup between them on the coffee table.

He moved the big tray, filled with the paltry remains of their breakfast, and he didn't try to hide a thing as he sat down where the tray had been.

"Oh," she said again, only breathlessly.

Carefully, he leaned forward and kissed her. She didn't taste like mint this time, but of coffee and jam. He knew she was still tender so he had to be cautious when caution was the last thing he wanted.

Her hand came up to his neck and she held him steady as she took the lead. It was a perfect solution.

She was the one to turn her head, to thrust her tongue into his mouth. She pressed him harder and he didn't hesitate to respond in kind.

Her soft moan made him hard all over again and so soon after his shower it made him grunt in surprise.

He had no idea what she made of the sound except that it brought her closer. So close, in fact, that without relinquishing the kiss, she somehow climbed right into his lap, her legs circling his waist.

It was no use trying not to touch her. His hand went to her back, only he didn't want to feel her T. He found the hem and snuck underneath and he was immediately rewarded with the softest thing he'd ever felt.

Mia moaned again as she ran her fingers through his hair, as she toyed with his tongue, as she wriggled on his lap.

He should stop this. Walk away while he still could. In a moment he was going to have no choice but to take her to that big white bed.

MIA COULDN'T GET close enough to him. Her hands were on his face, cupping the sides to hold him where she wanted him, and she kissed him deeply, holding back nothing. He cradled her perfectly on his lap with those big hands roaming across her back, and it felt so good, so right. She didn't even care about the twinges from her shoulder. They were nothing compared to finally, finally kissing him, feeling how much he wanted her.

Bax leaned back, pulled away from her greedy mouth. "Wait, stop."

Her whimper escaped before she could hide it. "No."

"I don't want to hurt you."

"You're not."

"But I will if I take you into the bedroom."

She looked at his concerned eyes, at the bit of moisture she'd left on his lips. "Let me worry about that."

He shook his head. "You're still healing. It's crazy."

She pushed off him and somehow got her legs under her as she stood. "You're right. It's crazy." Holding out her hand, she could see his dilemma written all over that rugged face.

She urged him on silently, willing him to feel how much she wanted this. Wanted him. And when he took her hand and stood up, the butterflies in her tummy leapt for joy.

"Mia, this is nuts. We can wait. Tomorrow, maybe, or the next day."

"Now." She pulled him with her to the bedroom door, then next to the bed.

"I'll feel like hell if I do something that hurts you."

She thought about arguing the point, but decided words wouldn't cut it. Instead, she grabbed the bottom of her sleep shirt and yanked the damn thing off.

He shut up right quick.

When she slid off her panties, he appeared to have forgotten how to talk.

Hiding her triumphant grin, she got busy taking off the detective's clothes. Her hands went to his shirt buttons and she undid them as quickly as her shaky fingers could.

By the time she got to his jeans, he lurched out of his fugue state and joined in on the fun. Balancing on one foot then the other he got his shoes off and maybe his socks, she didn't bother to look, not when she had to concentrate on undoing the next set of buttons.

He took over and there he was, as naked as she was, only he showed his enthusiasm in a much more vivid way.

She took a step toward him and after she'd captured his gaze, she ran the tip of her finger from the base to the crown of his cock.

His eyes fluttered shut as he groaned pitifully. It was wonderful.

"We can do this," she whispered into his neck. She nipped him there where she could reach without straining. "Let me show you."

His hands were on her back once more, only this time he didn't stop until he'd cupped her behind and drawn her close.

She felt the scratch of chest hair against her breasts, felt his weeping cock against her thigh. It was all wonderful, but not enough. She wiggled free and sat on the edge of the bed. "Lie down."

He looked at her sitting there, then got on the bed, on his knees, and then he maneuvered himself conveniently beside her, stretched out and gorgeous with his head neatly on the pillow.

She stood again, figuring her best approach. "You just stay still," she said, and laughed as she saw his hand, inches from his cock, freeze in midair.

Although she wanted to hurry, she forced herself to be careful. Now would be a tragic time to pull her stitches or fall on her head.

Her slow movements seemed to captivate her audience, so she relaxed, making it all work.

He was easy to straddle with those slim hips, and the view from on top was delicious. From the way he smiled, she gathered he'd seen the simplicity and economy of her position. He didn't have to worry now. She would control the pace and if she started to hurt then they'd rethink things.

But she wasn't going to hurt.

It was tempting, what with him being so hard and standing tall, so to speak, to back up and bend forward, but no. That would have to wait for another time. Right now, what she wanted was to go for a long, slow ride.

"You sure?" he asked.

"Surer than sure."

His smile broke. "Protection."

Disappointment hit, but only for a second as she remembered where they were. "We're in Hush."

"Yeah," he said, not catching on.

"Hush hotel." She pointed to the big armoire. "A full service hotel."

"The rooms come with condoms?"

"A wide assortment." She took his cock in her hand and gave it a little squeeze. "Don't go anywhere."

His hiss told her she needn't worry. Then it was all about the dismount and a quick, well, sort of, walk to the cupboard.

She flung the doors open to find a treasure chest full of naughty goodies. Furry handcuffs, dildos, vibrators, feathers, powder, videos, oh my, a whip which didn't look as if it was designed to really hurt, and much, much more. There, between the Astroglide and the edible panties was a basket of condoms. She hadn't exaggerated about the variety.

Not willing to waste another second, she grabbed the basket and went back to the bed. "Choose," she said, putting it down on his chest.

He didn't even look at the selection as she climbed back on top of him. He only had eyes for her.

Comfortably back in place after the delay, she made the choice herself, picking one packet at random.

She ditched the basket and tore the package, then proceeded to prepare him as her body let her know in no uncertain terms that she had to hurry.

She caught a glimpse of his white-knuckled fist. She wasn't the only impatient one.

"Finally," she said. "I've been wanting to do this for a long time."

Bax gurgled. No actual words came out and yet she understood perfectly. Holding him steady, she lifted herself up and aimed.

12

BAX WAS ON SENSUAL OVERLOAD. Shockingly, he was grateful for the condom. Maybe it would help him maintain a bit. Considering the fact that just her touch was enough to make him explode, it was a good thing.

God, just looking at her stunning body, naked and quivering above him like something sent from heaven. She was small all over, and that was fine with him. Her breasts, Jesus, they were perfect. Especially with her nipples hard and jutting.

He couldn't completely relax. Right next to his excitement was his concern. If he were a stronger man, he'd insist that they wait. At least with her on top, he could watch, make sure she wasn't in trouble.

She had him in a terrible position though. Holding his shaft had been bad enough, but now she was teasing him, rubbing the supersensitive glans up and down, making him shake with his need to thrust. He ground his teeth together, held on to the side of the bed and the sheets, praying for mercy.

Keeping his eyes open was another tortuous exercise. Not just because she was so beautiful it hurt, but because she knew exactly what she was doing to him, and she was having an enormously good time as she did it.

"Mia," he said, although it was more of a growl than a word.

"Is something wrong?"

"I'm begging."

"Hmm. I think I like that," she said, only he could hear the tremble in her voice.

"You'll be sorry when I have an aneurysm."

"Oh, it's not all that bad, is it?"

He meet her evil gaze. "It's worse."

Her smile softened just a bit. "Okay, sailor. You ask, I obey."

With that, she lowered herself slowly, achingly slowly, onto his cock.

It was indescribable. For a man who loved words, he had none. No language existed that was powerful enough, exciting enough, the sensations were that intense. To remain still as he filled her, as her hot velvet squeezed him, was impossible. He simply couldn't hold back.

At least he didn't let loose. If he had, she'd have sailed across the room. As it was, she had to find purchase on his chest.

He took hold of her slender, warm hips as he kept his pace slow and steady. She moaned the most erotic sound he'd ever heard, then found and captured his gaze.

"Oh, my God, Bax."

He lowered himself in that same excruciating pace.

"This is, oh, God, it's too much."

He froze as he was, stilling every part of him, including his breath. "Are you all right?"

"Don't stop. Don't you dare stop. I'm more than okay. I'm in a new dimension. I mean, oh. Oh. Shit."

Hearing her swear, even that mild curse, made his predicament worse. Whatever the condom was doing, it wasn't enough, because he was heading straight to blast-off.

He didn't want to go there, not yet. Not until she could blast off with him.

He let her go with his right hand, and moved that to where her body and his came together. It was exciting to touch the little bit of hair that covered her mound, but that wasn't the goal. One more shift and there, his finger slipped between her moist lips. Not too far. Just until he reached her clit.

"Oh, my—"

He knew he had it right when she lost the power of speech.

He stroked her, not too hard, but very fast. She increased her pace along with him. A moment later, her mouth opened wide, her eyes fluttered closed, and he felt the most exquisite pressure squeeze his buried cock.

His fingering stopped as his cock became the universe. Nothing existed outside of the pressure to come. He thrust up one last time, lifting Mia as she continued to squeeze.

He saw stars behind his eyelids, heard himself howl as if he'd been stabbed, shot, mangled, but instead of pain he was dying from the most shattering orgasm he'd ever experienced, and man, he'd had a lot.

Once the ringing in his ears became a dull roar he got to hear Mia's version of what it felt like to splinter into a million pieces of pleasure. She wasn't as loud and her cries were more delicate, but yeah, it was something. He kept having these tremors that were not as powerful but almost as sweet as coming.

Mia lowered her body until she was lying on his chest,

her head nestled in the crook of his shoulder. Bax put his arms around her, and soon, even their breaths were like one.

SHE REALLY NEEDED to move. Not because she wanted to leave him, but her right leg was cramping and she needed an aspirin for her head.

Totally worth it, though. In fact, she would have been willing to go through a lot more if the reward had been making love with Bax.

"Hey," she said, wondering if she was going to wake him.

"Hmm?"

"I've got to move. Just thought I'd warn you."

He sighed. "I supposed it is impractical to live the rest of our lives like this."

"Just a bit."

"Too bad," he said as he reluctantly moved his hands from her back.

She kissed his neck and sat up again. Something told her if she stayed like that, if she moved in the right way, he'd be raring to go, but he had things to do. Important things. Things that she would miss out on, being sequestered and all.

No, she wasn't even going to think about the case. She would take a really long bath. Then she'd watch TV, which she never did. Order room service. Call Carlane and Jenna and Moira and all her concierge pals to give them the scoop.

"You okay?"

She was still sitting on him. "Fine. Wonderful. Happy." She moved off him and the bed, and went to her purse to get the aspirin.

With a groan, Bax got out of bed, too, and headed straight for the bathroom. She heard the shower and debated joining him, but she'd made him late enough.

Despite her headache, she found herself grinning like a fool. She'd imagined being in bed with him a lot, but the real thing was so, so much better. She could hardly believe her luck. All those women out there who thought they were happy. They didn't know that she'd gotten the best one. The handsomest, smartest, sweetest, funniest…

Oh, my. Uh-huh. She had it bad. Really, really bad.

Behind her, she heard the soft padding of bare feet. Then felt hands on her shoulders. Lips on her neck. "Holy shit," he whispered.

She laughed, turning to face him. His hair was all damp and his skin glowed. She looked him over, appreciating more than ever what a low-slung towel around the hips could do for a man. "Can you call in sick?"

"I can," he said. "But I don't think it would be wise."

"Why not? Let someone else solve the crimes. We could order all the desserts on the room service menu. And dirty movies! We could watch a whole bunch of those."

"Stop, you're killing me. I have to get dressed. I have to do my duty."

"Duty, schmooty. I want you here."

He kissed her. "I want to be here. And I will be. Later."

"Stupid criminals."

"My thoughts exactly."

"All right. I'm going to take a bath."

"Good. Then get back in bed. Rest. I'm a terrible man for taking advantage of you in your weakened state. You must get well so I don't live the rest of my life under a pall of guilt."

"Very well. Just for you, I'll get better."

He kissed her once more.

Yep. She'd gotten the best one. No doubt about it.

IT WAS DIFFICULT for Bax to get back into the swing of things, but only for about ten minutes. It wasn't his devotion to duty that had him hunting for bear, either, but the idea that someone out there, someone he'd spoken to, smiled at, questioned, had tried to kill Mia.

There were still too many things he didn't know.

No time like the present to fix that. The moment he got to the lobby, he called Grunwald. Whoever and whatever was stalling the search warrant to Sheila Geiger's was going to get a rude awakening. After that was taken care of, Bax was going to pay a visit to Oscar Weinberg, and this time, Bax knew exactly what to look for.

DAYTIME TV WASN'T nearly as wonderful as Mia remembered. There were too many commercials and not enough Clive Owen for her taste.

She clicked off the gorgeous flat panel TV and went in search of her cell phone. What she needed was a fix.

"Ellen? It's Mia. Do me a favor? Find out if we have a free loaner laptop, okay? And could you ask Theresa, if she has a minute, to bring it to suite 1406?"

"Well, yes, of course, I can, but sweetie, you have to spill. What in the world happened to you yesterday? It's all over the Internet."

"What?"

"Did you think it wouldn't get noticed? The Golden Key is all abuzz."

The Golden Key was the premiere concierge association,

and practically everyone Mia knew was a member. Including her parents. "I'll give you the whole scoop, but not right now. I have to call my folks. They must be going insane."

"Later," Ellen said.

Mia hung up and for the next half an hour she in turn apologized profusely and reassured first her mother then her father, then her mother all over again. A knock on the door saved her from round three.

It was Theresa. And Ellen. And the laptop.

Mia ushered them in, where both women oohed and aahed over her impressive bruise and her stitches. Then they had to know every little thing that happened in the garage.

Theresa was completely sure that Oscar Weinberg pulled the trigger. Ellen's money was on Bobbi Tamony. Mia kept her opinion to herself, although she was both wheedled and cajoled.

Finally, though, she was on her own again and connected to the outside world. With her phone in one hand and her other on the trackball mouse, she was all set. She would get through the day without going insane. She would stay put, and not get into trouble. What she wouldn't do was stop trying to solve the murder of Gerry Geiger.

OSCAR WAS IN HIS SUITE, which was just where Bax wanted him. He was spread out in the living room like a maharaja, with a bowl of fruit at his fingertips, a speakerphone blaring, and three, count them, three assistants in a worshipful circle before him, writing down every word that was uttered.

Bax was happy to wait, but he wasn't about to sit in his assigned chair. He needed to find the camera. Cameras.

There wasn't a chance in hell Oscar hadn't had them installed. One was undoubtedly on his desk, but he needed more. He needed to get a good view of every possible visitor, in every possible location. The man was a film producer and he knew about coverage.

When they made a movie, they used one camera, and kept moving it to get all the angles necessary. But in a static location, like the suite, Oscar would have to have planted cameras all over the place, just in case.

So Bax wandered around the perimeter of the living room. He knew Oscar was dying to make him sit. To make him stop. Even though the room had to be in the low seventies, Oscar had a budding garden of sweat on his face, and his eyes, those beady green eyes, they were captivated.

Bax was enjoying this, especially knowing that Grunwald and Miguel were on their way to Sheila Geiger's with a great big old search warrant. By the time he finished with Oscar, the boys should be at the precinct, cataloging every picture, memory card, camera and computer.

"Detective," Oscar said, shutting down the speakerphone. "Have a seat."

"Thanks," Bax said, but he didn't even look at the chair. Instead, he picked up an ornate box sitting on a credenza. "I have a few questions for you, Mr. Weinberg."

"No problem. You want some coffee? Maybe something cooler?"

"I'm good," Bax said, as if he were talking to a friend. Or at the very least someone he could stand. "You told me before that from time to time you'd hire Gerry Geiger to take some pictures." Bax put the box down now that he'd seen the tiny little hole in the side. "Yeah, that's right. You hired Geiger quite often. But you said you didn't call him personally, is that correct?"

"Yes, that's correct."

Bax meandered further, to a big flower arrangement at the other end of the credenza. The flowers, he realized after touching one, were fake. Not something that would have been provided by Hush. There wasn't a fake flower anywhere in this hotel. "So who did?" he asked.

"Who did what?" Oscar mopped his face with a small white handkerchief.

Bax hadn't realized men still carried handkerchiefs. "Who made the calls to Geiger? Which one of your…associates?"

"I don't know. Whoever was handy."

"Really? And you didn't worry that the word would get out? That you were paying Geiger for capturing your stars on film? That some of those pictures had the potential to destroy your stars' careers? You trusted whoever was handy to keep that information quiet?"

"We aren't talking state secrets here, Detective. It's tabloid fodder. Publicity."

"Ah, but the right publicity can do so much. It can make or break a film. Or a star. If it were my picture, my movie stars, I'd be pretty damn careful who knew I was manipulating the media. Damn careful."

"Well, they weren't your pictures, Detective."

"You're right. They weren't. So I imagine I'll be way the hell off base when I ask Nan Collins about calling Gerry Geiger for you. Or when I ask her about what favors she did for you in Mexico."

Oscar was a smooth operator, but there was just enough of a pause that Bax knew he'd hit pay dirt.

"Nan Collins is a two-bit actress who would be collecting unemployment if it wasn't for me. Between films she does some grunt work. Nothing special."

"So, she didn't do anything special in Mexico."

"I have no idea what you're talking about, Detective. And if you don't have anything more specific to discuss, I'm going to have to ask you to leave. I'm a busy man."

"I'm a busy man, too, Oscar. For example, I'm going from here to speak to your massage therapist, Larry. He called me last night. Said he wants to chat. And then, oh, man, then I'm really going to be swamped because we picked up all the cameras and all the memory cards and pictures from Gerry Geiger's place. The warrant, let me see, yeah, the warrant was for the house, the basement, the garage and you know that little shed he kept in the back? For there, too."

Oscar stood, and the three transcribing monkeys froze like a tableau. No one moved except the big man. He walked over to Bax and the little beads of sweat trembled. "I asked you very nicely to leave, Detective, and when you do, I'm going to make a phone call."

"To Nan?"

"To the mayor of this fair city. He's a personal friend. Nice guy. Owes me a favor."

"I'd probably be worried about that if I hadn't already turned in my resignation. I'm leaving, you know. Going back to school. Can't wait."

"Well, I still think the mayor will be interested in what I have to tell him. I know he's good friends with Piper Devon. The owner of this hotel. If I happen to mention that there was an incident in my room with a certain attractive concierge, it's hard to say what his reaction would be."

Bax smiled. "No skin off my nose."

"No? I don't believe you, Detective."

"Believe what you want. If she gets fired, she'll get another job."

From the look of Oscar's jaw, he wasn't pleased with the direction of the conversation. "She won't be finding another job, Detective. Not in this city or any other."

"So, if I drop this, you'll let my friend be, right?"

Oscar sighed. "Are you always this dense, or is this a special treat for me? Yes, that's right."

Bax very purposefully stepped to his right, his hip hitting the credenza so hard he'd have a bruise. But it was worth it, because the fake flower arrangement fell to the floor and the ceramic crashed and splintered into a hundred pieces. And there, in the middle of the fake moss and plastic flowers, was a small video camera, its red light blinking as it continued to record.

"Well, now that's interesting," Bax said, as he bent to get the camera. "And convenient as all hell. Here I was going to have to take your three scribes down to the precinct to testify that you bribed a police officer. Now they don't have to go, because, damn, this little camera probably caught every word on tape."

"That's mine, Detective."

"Sorry. Plain sight. Probable cause. It was yours, Oscar. Now it's evidence. You have the right to remain silent…"

MIA WAS DRESSED in a stunning Stella McCartney white mini that hugged whatever curves there were, and made the straight parts seem less important. The shoes should have been four-inch stilettos, but all Mia had were some black ballet flats. Never mind, she still felt fabulous. It didn't matter that half her face was mostly purpley-blue.

Or that she couldn't shrug without whimpering. The only thing that counted was that Bax was coming. Soon.

She checked out the living room, hoping against hope he'd be happy with what she'd done. It wasn't interfering. It was helping.

The big whiteboard? That was courtesy of catering. They'd brought the easel and the board and all the fun-colored marking pens about three hours earlier.

Mia had done a timeline, starting with the shoot in Mexico, then jumping six years to the night of Gerry Geiger's murder. She'd written down everything she knew for a fact in black. Everything she'd heard secondhand in blue. Everything she guessed in red. There wasn't much black.

But she didn't know everything Bax knew, and there were still three colors left.

She checked the clock again. Only ten minutes had passed since his call. He'd been at the precinct going over pictures from the Geiger's house. It drove her crazy that she couldn't see them, too.

On the other hand, she might simply attack him at the door, and not come up for air 'til morning.

13

IT WAS A TOTAL REVELATION to come back to the suite and find Mia waiting for him.

First, the kissing. Frankly, he'd always considered the kissing as the girly part. Not that he didn't enjoy the process, but it had never been the goal. He supposed that it wasn't the goal now, either, but if that was all they could do, just kiss all night, it would have been okay. Better than okay.

Then there was just the fact that she was so excited to see him. Talk about a rush. Even in the beginning of his relationship with Carol there hadn't been this electricity on either of their parts. It astonished him that he had this much excitement in him.

Then Mia had got the whiteboard. Well, damn, that was just beyond belief. Just looking at it, at her, made him remember why he'd wanted to become a cop in the first place. He'd wanted *this*. Stimulating conversation, having a partner who was clever as well as logical, solving crimes that would stymie everyone else. Who'd have guessed he'd find his ideal partner in this plucky, beautiful concierge.

While he read all her brightly colored points, she ordered them dinner, then came over to read with him.

"Did you see the pictures?" she asked as she slipped her right hand into his back pocket so she could cup his ass.

"Yeah, I did. Most, at least. There were a few cameras that still had film that needed to be developed. But we got everything that had been loaded onto the computers, and we took a quick look at the pictures on the memory cards. There weren't nearly enough."

"You mean there weren't enough pictures or pictures that help with the case?"

"Both. No way Geiger made a living on the pictures we saw. They were all either mundane or out of focus or both. Lots of pictures of Nan, though. It made me wonder if she and Gerry had something going on."

Mia's other hand went to his chest and she rubbed him as she read the board. "She is all over the place, isn't she? But—"

"What? he asked, pulling her closer.

"It struck me this afternoon as I was talking to Carlane. You know, my tabloid expert? When I asked her about Nan, she'd never heard of her. Never seen anything mentioned about Nan."

Bax nodded. He'd heard she was a glorified extra. That she worked for Weinberg between films. Why would she be in the rags?

And why would she turn down a recurring role in a popular TV series?

The answer was that she wouldn't. Unless she had no choice.

"This whole mess can be summed up with one word," Bax said. "Blackmail."

Mia nodded. "The question, though, is who was doing the blackmailing and for what ultimate end?"

"Not to mention, who would need to have Gerry Geiger out of the way. Why not just shoot Weinberg?"

"For what it's worth, I don't think the killer was Danny Austen, even if Sheila Geiger thinks so."

"Why not?"

"Well, for an actor, he seems pretty happy."

"Huh?"

"Bobbi Tamony isn't. The only thing she gets any pleasure from, in my not so humble opinion, is her dogs. She doesn't like what she's doing, she doesn't like the people she's with. That's why she does the drugs."

"And Danny?"

"He jokes a lot, flirts a lot. Evidently, he sleeps with whomever he wants. Even when I caught him in the shower, he was surprised, but I don't know. He didn't seem like he wanted to kill me."

"Do you think Bobbi could have done it?"

"Nope. My money's on Oscar, or Oscar by way of Nan."

He turned to her, pulling her close against his chest. "You know, they're going to be one detective short in a few months over at Midtown. You're a natural."

She sighed. "No thanks. I like my mysteries to be more like treasure hunts. With no dead bodies as the prize."

"Smart, smart woman."

"And you're smart to get out while you still have dreams."

"Naturally," he said, "the most interesting case of my career comes up now."

"Naturally. It's a test from the gods. They want to make sure you're meant to leave."

Bax studied her for a long moment as he fought the urge to tell her he wasn't going. That he felt reborn, renewed. That leaving her would be the cruelest of ironies.

But he wasn't sure if all that was true, or if he was simply in the throes of a new-relationship brain fog. Was it even possible to fall in love with someone so quickly? Not lust, that was a given, but real love? The kind that lasted till the end of days?

It felt as if that was exactly what he'd found. He just wished he could trust his emotions.

"I think I am meant to leave," he said. "Not that I relish leaving you."

He could tell she'd hoped for a different answer. Her smile had dimmed, but she still wore her game face.

"I have to tell you the truth," she said. "Not that I want you to change your plans—okay, maybe that's not completely true. I want you to be happy and fulfilled and to love your job the way I love mine. But the thought of saying goodbye—"

He bent for another kiss. The conversation had taken some of the zip out of the air, but it was good to know how she felt. Wouldn't it just be something if the two of them…

No, that was crazy. Real life didn't work like the movies. He broke the kiss but not his hold on Mia. "What if Nan had to turn down the role because Oscar has pictures of her that are so damning, she'd face a life in prison if they got out? What would a person do to avoid that?"

"Especially if the prison were in Mexico. Do they have a statute of limitations?"

"Doubt it. Especially not for murder."

Room service interrupted, but pleasantly so. After paying the young man who seemed to like Mia too much, Bax set them up on the coffee table. He poured Mia a cold tea, then made sure she'd taken her pills, which, no, she hadn't since she didn't need to until bedtime.

Then they attacked their dinners. Her with salmon, him with a ribeye, and both of them lost in a curious mix of murder, blackmail and the certainty that soon there would be mind-blowing sex.

"How do we get proof on any of this?" Mia asked.

"*We* don't get anything. I will figure out a way."

"Yeah, yeah," Mia said. "Question. Was part of Nan's job for Weinberg to tip off Geiger?"

"I think so, yes."

"And you said something about Geiger and Nan having an affair."

"I have nothing to substantiate that. Nothing."

"But it does put the two of them together. And I know Sheila thinks Geiger and Danny were doing it, but what if it was really Nan and Geiger? And say that Sheila's been taking these phone calls from this chick for years. Then she finds a picture of the two them doing the deed. I'd think she'd be pretty darn miffed."

"Especially if she knew her husband was planning on leaving her."

"So Sheila kills her husband? Knowing he's at Hush because Nan called?"

Bax thought about it as he chewed. "Something that bothers me. The murder was well thought-out. Whoever killed Geiger really thought things through. You'd be amazed at the lack of physical evidence. Killing Geiger in the night-club was smart. Too many fingerprints to use anything. No murder weapon. No blood, except for Geiger's. No trace under his fingernails. Anyway, Sheila doesn't strike me as the ideal candidate. First, she'd have to have been sober."

"And not just during the murder, but to plan it. That doesn't seem right."

"And I don't believe Oscar would ever deign to kill someone with his own hands." Bax thought of those three uncomfortable stenos sitting like begging puppies waiting for a bone. "I think he used his most vulnerable lapdog."

"Nan."

"It all comes around to her, doesn't it?"

"I wish we had more information about the Mexico thing," Mia said. "Why would Nan tie the girl up? That seems weird."

Bax nodded. "I have no idea. I've done a lot of studying in my time about the criminal mind. Honest. I know more about warped individuals than most people. More than is good for me. But when I get among the movie people, all my studying isn't worth beans. They throw off the bell curve in a major way."

"Yeah. I agree. It's not just because they're rich, either. Because I see lots of rich people."

"I think it's because anyone crazy enough to be in the movies is crazy enough to do anything."

She smiled. She didn't say anything at all. She just smiled this sweet smile all for him.

Finally, when he thought maybe he should start worrying, she said, "I enjoy you so much. You're like the most interesting kid in the class, the one who's all mysterious and weird because he's read every book in the library. Only you're hot, too!"

He burst out laughing. She laughed, too, but not because she'd been joking. If that's what she thought of him, he could do a lot worse.

He also noticed she was moving a lot more freely today. Her shoulder didn't seem to bother her much at all, and despite the ugly bruise, it appeared her head wasn't that bad, either. "You aren't hurting?"

She shrugged, but only with her good shoulder. "Not so much. I've taken a few aspirin and those have helped a lot."

"That's good. That's great."

"Yeah," she said as she folded her napkin and put it on her plate. "In fact…"

"Yes?"

"I was thinking that you could, if you wanted to, fill in the blanks on the board. Which shouldn't take all that long, right?"

"Hardly any time at all."

"Good. Then we could do some research."

"Oh?" He didn't let his voice show his disappointment.

She lowered her head and looked at him through her lashes. "There's that whole big armoire in the bedroom. Chock-full of interesting things to play with."

He leaned back on the couch. "And you expect me to work now that you've planted that little gem in my brain?"

"Who, me?" she said so innocently he had to laugh again.

He put his dinner on the room service cart, added hers, then pushed the whole thing into the hallway. Since he was staying the night, he'd convinced Piper to let the security guard leave, so there was no one in the hall.

When he closed and locked the door, Mia was nowhere to be seen. Which could only mean she was already in the bedroom.

As much as exploring the armoire excited him, he had to keep Mia's health in mind. She might feel fine, but that didn't mean she was. No gymnastics, then. No out-there fetish stuff that would them ache in the morning. He'd keep things nice. Sensual.

Barely giving the whiteboard a glance, he headed straight for the bedroom. A quick wash-up and tooth cleaning and he'd be ready for action.

But then, he'd have to be able to walk past an incredibly

gorgeous, extremely naked Mia, lying on the bed like the most perfect gift ever.

"I was going to—" He pointed toward the bathroom.

"Go. I'll be here when you're done."

"But—"

"Bax, go. I want everything perfect for both of us."

"You are."

She smiled. "Okay, you get extra points for that one, but still. Do what you need to do. I'll be thinking of all the things I want to do to you."

He groaned halfway to the bathroom, and once there he got cleaned up in record time. He stripped there, too, not wanting to waste a moment of being with Mia.

"Do you want to make out for awhile?" she asked. "Or go into the armoire first?"

What he wanted was to do both at the same time, but he went to the armoire. Not to explore so much as to find something he guessed would be there. And it was. He took his prize and the basket of condoms, and joined her.

Mia didn't even look at what he'd brought. She just pulled him down to the pillows, to her kisses.

SHE LOVED HIS MOUTH. His lips. His teeth. It was crazy how she couldn't get enough of kissing him. And touching him. Yes. Touching while kissing. That was the ideal combo. A little nip on the jaw or the neck for added spice, but mostly she could kiss and touch all night long.

Oh, until he touched her there. Whoa.

"You okay?" he mumbled, his lips still on hers.

"Uh-huh."

No words could escape for the next while, but then Bax

pulled back and after a deep breath, he said, "Mia, you make me insane."

"In a good way."

"Oh, yeah."

Then his fingers slipped inside her once more and she realized that whatever other talents he might have, he should be most proud of this. He knew just how hard to push, how gently to rub, and he had the build-to-a-climax thing down pat.

"What are you doing?" she asked. "I swear I'm going to come if you don't stop."

"Good," he said, pushing his two fingers into her like a little jackhammer as his thumb circled and circled her clit until she was gasping for breath. Until all the muscles in her body became taut.

And then he stopped.

She hit him in the chest. Hard. "Hey!"

He shook his head. "Do you really think I'm going to leave you like this? Huh?"

"No."

"Well, then?"

She sighed. And lay back. "Okay then."

He chuckled as he retrieved the box he'd taken from the armoire.

"What is that?"

"You'll see. But later. Right now, I want you to close your eyes and relax."

"I assume you want me to keep them closed."

"Yes. Keep them closed."

"It's going to be wonderful, isn't it?" she asked as she obeyed. "I'm going to love it, aren't I?"

"Yes, and yes. Now, shh. Let it happen."

She heard him futzing with cellophane, then more futzing with something she couldn't identify, something torn, and then… "Oh, my."

He laughed again, low, slow. But it was whatever was in his hand that had her squirming. The softest feeling in the world, like feathers, only better. A brush, only more delicate and heavenly, sweeping across her thighs, her belly. Unable to resist, she spread her legs and because he was so wonderful the brush went to the sensitive skin of her inner thighs then across the lips, then back to her belly. It was a sensual delight including the scent of sweet seduction. Almonds? Roses? Yes, and spices she wasn't familiar with, but that made her sigh with pleasure.

For a long time, she felt suspended in a cloud. He painted her with magic dust and every part of her felt shimmery and tantalized.

When he took the brush away, she whimpered even knowing he was going to give her something more. Something better.

Another moment, and then his fingers were once more at the junction of her thighs. He parted her lips and rubbed her clit, only as he circled so gently it made her wriggle, there was something more, not just his finger. Oil. Warmth. A new scent, like flowers.

A moment later, she felt his breath on her breast, his moist tongue on her nipple. All the while he kept circling with that heat. It was just right, just hot enough to make things interesting, to make her slide right back to that magic space where coming was inevitable.

Her gasps were quicker now and he sucked her nipples, each one in turn, harder and harder until she was arching her back demanding more.

He never stopped rubbing her, even when she felt his knees push her thighs further apart, and his lips left her nipples wet and hard.

She grabbed his shoulders, grabbed the bed as she got closer and closer, her legs stiff, her toes pointed, and she was there…there…

"Oh, Bax." She bucked as she came, as her whole body thrilled to the rise and release and before she could even catch her breath, there was more. There was Bax.

He lifted her legs and pushed them back in a move that stole the cry from her lips. He thrust inside her, hard and deep as he filled her with his cock, and she came again, which she hadn't expected because she'd never, ever felt like this.

He pumped into her like a wild man and it was perfect. Amazing, and she didn't care that it ached when her head rolled on the pillow because it was so good, so good.

She felt his arms tremble, heard his grunts as he took her, and that was it, she had to open her eyes.

He was over her, his dark hair wild, his eyes wilder, and the hunger he had for her distorting his face. Stripping the civilized veneer away and leaving the animal at her gate.

She wanted to touch him, to feel his muscles bulge and lick the sweat from his arms, but she was helpless, her body captive as he turned her into a madwoman.

She still quivered as he grimaced, as his thrusts became shorter, erratic. And then he cried out in a howl of purest pleasure as he came.

When he finally let her go, she was wasted. A puddle of goo without a coherent thought except that she couldn't let this man go. Not tonight, not tomorrow. Not ever.

14

As soon as Mia closed the door behind Bax her smile faded and she turned to face her luxurious prison. If a person had to stay inside, this was surely the place to do it, but it was still inside.

The thing was, she felt fine. More than fine. The magic healing power of great sex gave her energy to burn. Talking about the case, having Bax truly listen and consider her opinions made her desperate to get out there, do something. Anything that would help.

So she couldn't go out in person, but she could extend her eyes and ears over Manhattan.

First thing, a shower, which was no minor activity. Not when the shower in question had four different kinds of spray, from the big rainfall drops to a long vertical massaging spray to go up and down the spine. Then there was the soap and shampoo and conditioner and moisturizer, all of which were made by an astonishing family business upstate. Everything they made was full of herbs and aloe and all manner of good things which made the products and the lucky person using them smell as good as a person could.

She gave herself permission to linger, to let herself daydream about Bax. She pretended he was going to stay, that she was enough to keep him here. And that staying with her would make him so happy he'd forget all about Boulder and teaching. He'd write, though, with her as his muse. They'd solve crimes together and make love at the drop of a hint, and they'd love each other so much.

The picture she painted was perfect. Idyllic. Even though she understood it wasn't going to come true, she wasn't going to stop dreaming it until she had to. There was plenty of time to be sad later, when he was really gone. No use jumping ahead, starting the sadness now. This was the best part. When they were still in the discovery phase, and a person would have to be a masochist to miss this by filling her brain with things that might go wrong.

Today, she had Bax. She had her health. She had a world class suite to stay in. A job she loved. Friends all over the city. Family who adored her.

And to top it all off, she smelled good enough to eat.

As she dressed, she thought about what more she could do. Carlane would help, as usual. But first, Mia had to figure out a way to get a picture of Sheila Geiger. Bax would think of something.

"WHAT EXACTLY DO YOU need her picture for?"

Bax hadn't left the building. He'd tried to find Nan Collins, but she wasn't anywhere around, and she wasn't picking up her cell. Danny Austen had agreed to meet him at two, Larry the massage guy at three, and he was waiting to hear back from Grunwald about the video he'd taken from Oscar Weinberg.

"Nothing illegal or immoral," Mia said. "I just want to see if Carlane knows anything about her."

"There were some pictures of her in that bunch we got yesterday. I'll have Miguel send one over."

"He can e-mail it to me."

Bax gave her Miguel's cell number. "Tell him what you want. He'll get right on it."

"He won't think it's weird? Some strange girl calling for a favor?"

Bax grinned. "Fishing, are we?"

"Who, me?"

"I may have mentioned your name to Miguel. And Grunwald."

"What did you tell them?"

"Nothing private or personal."

"Then they don't know you can't keep your hands off me?"

He leaned back in his chair, debating going right back upstairs. "No, and they don't need to. We're professionals, Mia. We don't gossip like schoolgirls."

Mia gasped. "I'm shocked that you would lie to me like that."

"Who, me?" he said, echoing her tone exactly.

"I have phone calls to make," she said. "But no one up here would have any objections to you coming for lunch. Or a snack."

"Tempting," he said. "Very tempting."

"If you knew how good I smelled, you'd be here already."

Bax closed his eyes and moaned. "Stop."

"Okay. Sorry. Be safe."

Bax put his phone down, and briefly toyed once more with going up to 1406, but then he thought about the whiteboard and how things were finally taking shape in the investigation. The best thing he could do was keep the pressure on. Oscar knew he wasn't kidding around. It wouldn't surprise Bax if Nan was on to him, too. He agreed with Mia about Danny and Bobbi, but now that he had more information, his questioning might lead somewhere.

His day was chock-full of being a detective. But the minute he was off the clock…

IT WAS ALMOST NOON, and Mia had just called down for a big salad and iced tea as she waited for someone, anyone, to call.

Miguel had turned out to be a doll. He e-mailed her a bunch of Sheila pictures and threw in four of Nan as a bonus. Mia in turn had sent the e-mails to several concierges in hotels nearby with instructions to notify her immediately if either woman was spotted.

Mostly, she wanted to know what Sheila was up to. The woman was still pursuing her lawsuit with Hush even though she had no chance of winning. Perhaps she hoped Piper would settle, rather than go to the trouble of a trial.

But she'd also been the one who'd planted the Mexico seed in Mia's head. Why? What did Sheila know about Mexico? She'd been married to Gerry at the time, so maybe she'd been in Mexico herself. There was no reason for Mexico to have been brought up at all, except to get someone in trouble. Maybe more than one someone.

Bax had said the pictures he'd gotten from the Geiger had numbered in the hundreds, and hadn't been the kind of photos the tabloids paid for. So where were the rest of the photos?

Was it possible Sheila was the real blackmailer? That Oscar was in cahoots with her, and when Gerry found out, they'd decided to have him killed?

She wasn't at all sure her shout-out to the concierge community would bear any fruit, but then, she knew damn well if there was a mystery afoot, the concierge gang would be all over it. They'd research, they'd dig, they'd cajole.

Hell, she'd done it often herself. She'd never tried to solve a murder, but she had helped Dean Schaeffer, the concierge at the Mandarin, get out of a very tight spot by proving a guest who had checked in under a false ID was the one who had stolen thousands of dollars' worth of antiques from the hotel.

She stared at the whiteboard, a veritable banquet of suspects, all of them with something to gain by Gerry Geiger's death.

It chilled her to think one of them was a cold-blooded killer. That one of them had aimed a gun at her and pulled the trigger.

There was simply no way she was going to sit idly by and let the killer go free. It might be more difficult, being confined to the suite, but not impossible.

DANNY AUSTEN HAD a Bloody Mary for lunch. Bax had the strong impression that the drink was an attempt to ease some of the ache from last night's excesses, especially after Danny had begged him to stop screaming. Bax figured he'd just whisper for the rest of the interview.

"There's food." Danny nodded gingerly toward the table by the couch, which was covered with platters of everything from fresh fruit to cold cuts to shrimp on ice. "Eat some."

"Thanks anyway, but I need to ask you some questions."

"I didn't do it," he said, wincing at his own words. "I told you."

"Tell me what happened in Mexico."

Danny's head snapped up, which evidently was a mistake, given his moan. "Mexico?"

"Come on, Danny. You're not in any condition to lie. So just tell me."

"There's nothing to tell."

"Right. So that girl who died, that was just an accident."

Danny stared at him, his bloodshot eyes full of fear.

"And, oh, how's that being blackmailed working out for you?"

Danny tossed the celery stalk to the carpet, then swallowed the rest of his drink in three gulps.

"I know he's got you on sleeping with guys," Bax said. "But hell, that doesn't seem like the biggest secret in the world. So what else does Oscar know?" Bax leaned forward. "What did Gerry Geiger photograph that's got you so scared you're willing to make this movie for peanuts. What kind of picture could be so damaging it could ruin your career?"

"You don't know who you're messing with," Danny said. "It's not what you think."

"Explain it to me."

Danny looked at the picture on the wall. It was him, of course, smiling that famous smile on some red carpet. He sighed with a tiredness that Bax felt from four feet away. "You know, I think it wouldn't be all that bad to have this career ruined."

"Mia, guess what?"

"Jenna?"

"Guess who's sitting in the bar right this very second?"

"No. Is it Sheila Geiger?"

"It is. She's three sheets to the wind, she's got a large suitcase by her side, and guess who she's with?"

"Who?"

"Okay, now I know you've hurt your head." Jenna sighed. "She's with her BFF Nan."

"What?"

"Although from the loudness, I'm guessing they won't be BFFs for long."

"They're fighting?"

"They are."

"Jenna, this is huge. Keep watching them. Don't lose them. Seriously. Someone will be right there."

"Someone? Who—"

But Mia was already speed dialing Bax. Who didn't answer. She hung up just as voice mail picked up. Then she dialed again. "Bax, Sheila and Nan are at the Algonquin bar. They're arguing. It sounds serious. You have to get there before they leave. Follow them.

Now, Bax. It's happening now!"

Then she hung up, not in the least sure what the hell she should do.

"Oh. Carlane." She dialed her friend's cell, pretty sure it was her day off.

"Hey, Mia."

"Carlane, I need you to do something, so please, please tell me you're not busy."

"It depends what you mean by busy. I'm shopping for shoes I can't afford."

"In the city?"

"Yeah, what's up?"

"Nan and Sheila Geiger are both at the bar at the Algonquin. I can't leave, Bax isn't answering his phone and I can't afford to lose them. They're arguing, and I just know they're going to bolt. Can you get there and follow them until I hear from Bax?"

"Holy crap, yes. I'm five minutes away. I'll call you the second I make contact."

"Okay, but be careful."

Carlane dismissed her with a girly grunt, then disconnected.

Mia dialed Jenna. "Carlane's coming. She's going to follow them."

"Mia, stop. I'm with a guest."

She waited, not even a little patiently. The only reason she wasn't going completely insane was that she had call waiting, so if Bax tried to reach her, he could.

And where the heck was he? She tried to remember what he'd told her about his afternoon. He was going to talk to Danny, then the masseur, then—

"Okay, I'm back. How long till she gets here? The tension in the bar is starting to get out of hand."

"Did you hear what they were arguing about?"

"Nope. Not a word. There's just much arm flailing and viciousness."

"Look, I'm going to call Bax again. I'll talk to you as soon as Carlane gets there."

"Got it."

Mia dialed immediately. After three rings, she gave up, staring at the phone as if it had betrayed her.

For the next five minutes, she paced the length of the living room, all the while trying to figure out what could have brought Sheila and Nan together. Was it because of the pictures? Bax had said there were a ton of Nan. Was Sheila trying to frame Nan? It made sense if Nan had been sleeping with Gerry. But how would Nan know what pictures had been removed from the house?

The whiteboard wasn't helping. Mia sat down, trying to find some calm. Even if Carlane lost them, so what? Just knowing that the two women were together and that they were arguing had to be a big plus. Despite being stuck in this room, she'd already helped. She had. It wasn't exactly an answer, but it was another clue. They were starting to add up.

Her phone rang, which made her jump. Praying it was Bax, she flicked it open. "Hello?"

"It's me," Carlane said. "I'm here."

"Thank heavens. Are they still arguing?"

"They are. But, according to Jenna, things have winded way down. I don't think they'll— Wait, they're going. One of them is going, at least. Nan. She just threw down some money on the table and she's standing. Saying something to Sheila, and yep, she's heading out."

"Follow her! Please. And ask Jenna to call me. Thanks, Carlane, and keep your distance. She could be really dangerous. And call."

She hung up, but not before Mia heard that rude noise again.

A few seconds later, Jenna was on the line. "Hey, what now?"

"Sheila's still there?"

"Yeah. She ordered another drink."

"Jenna, can you get away? I mean now?"

There was a long pause, which told Mia all she needed to know. "I'm sorry, hon, but there's no way. We're short staffed here and I'm on until at least six."

"Okay. No problem. I'll think of something."

"I'll let you know if anything happens."

"Okay, thanks. You're a star."

"WEINBERG, HE TAPED everything," Danny said. "He set up these parties, brought the drugs, brought all the hungry pretty people he could buy. We were young and hungry, too, and he made us feel like we were family, you know?

Me, Bobbi, Peter. We thought we were on a one-way trip to everything we'd ever dreamed of.

"So he'd lure us into situations that would make us look unreliable or uninsurable, or hell, put us in jail, then make sure he had evidence, courtesy of his pal Gerry Geiger. He figured he owned us, and he was right."

"Geiger was working for Weinberg?"

Danny nodded. "One of the nice little tricks Weinberg had was to make sure Geiger had access to us all. We never knew when Geiger would show up, where he was lurking. I'd come back from the set, and he'd be in my room. Camera at the ready. We all tried to make sure there was nothing going on that was worth photographing, but that never stopped him. He'd manufacture the photo ops."

"Like what?"

"Peter. He was photographed sleeping with a major producer's underage daughter. Bobbi had a taste for coke and Southern Comfort. She was in a couple of car wrecks. Of course, this was before going to jail was considered a good PR move. Me, well, you can guess."

"What about Nan?"

Danny sat back. Despite all he'd just spilled, Bax could see he wasn't quite ready to go there.

"Did you know that Nan was offered a recurring role on one of those *Law and Order* series?"

"No shit. Good for her."

"She turned it down."

Danny chewed on that for a bit. When he spoke again, it was softly, but with a lot of punch.

"DO YOU KNOW ANYONE at all who can go after her?" Mia stared out the window in the general direction of the Algonquin. It wasn't that far, for a person who could leave the room.

"I've asked, I've cajoled. Sweetie, I don't know what to tell you."

"I just can't… I even called the police station, but Miguel, he's the guy who e-mailed the pictures, he couldn't leave. He couldn't reach Bax, either, but he said if he didn't hear from him within the hour, he'd send out a unit. So now I'm freaked about Bax and about losing Sheila."

"Look, if I could—"

"I'm coming," Mia said, knowing she had no choice. "Keep her there, okay? Do whatever you have to, just make sure she doesn't get away."

"Mia. What the hell?"

"I'll see you in a few minutes." She hung up. Gave herself a good talking-to, every reason she should stay put and not follow Sheila. She called Bax one more time, left him yet another urgent message, then went into the bedroom to get changed.

15

MIA STEPPED INTO the hallway and found herself facing a very surprised security guard. She smiled brightly. "You're still here."

"Uh, yeah," the guard said. He was young, early twenties and she hadn't seen him before.

"I guess you haven't heard. They caught her."

"Who?"

"Sorry, I'm just excited. I was so afraid this was going to be a long, drawn-out affair. They caught the woman who took the shot at me. I'm going to the police station right now to make an ID."

"Nobody called me."

"This all just came down. You should probably call your boss. Anyway, thanks very much for making me feel so safe."

"You're welcome."

She headed down the hall after a brief wave and another smile. "Have a good day."

Maintaining her happy demeanor was tough while she waited for the elevator. Not because she'd just lied to the nice man, but because she had no desire to die. She'd gone over her plan several times, although one more time wouldn't hurt. She was going to the Algonquin, then she would follow Sheila at a very safe distance just until she heard from Bax. He'd zoom to her side, take her place, and she'd be back at Hush with no one the wiser. Except the security guard. That wasn't a big issue. She'd simply say that she'd been misinformed, sorry for the confusion.

No, the big issue had to do with being shot.

The big question was if she was being a complete moron.

Several stops later, she landed in the lobby. This was it, either she turned around right now, or hurried like hell.

If she turned back, they'd lose sight of Sheila. Which meant they'd have no idea where she was heading with that big suitcase. Mia would bet everything that suitcase was full of photos. Pictures that would solve the case.

Could she live with herself if she let those slip away?

She headed for the garage, although she didn't go to the northern exit. Instead, she hurried to Madison Avenue. All she had to do was get to East 44th Street, then turn left. A few blocks and she'd be at the Algonquin. Maybe by then, Bax would have called her back.

The film company was still there but they must have been shooting downstairs because none of the actors' chairs were around. There was a coffee setup, though, probably for the crew members who were waiting in their trucks for something to happen. She wondered if she'd spoken to, say, the script supervisor, maybe the whole mystery of the blackmail would have been revealed. If movie crews were anything like hotel staff, then they knew everything and then some.

She kept going, walking, jogging, but mostly walking because when she hit the pavement too hard it made her head hurt.

On East 44th, she stopped at a drugstore and bought herself a floppy-brimmed hat. It was actually pretty cute, and in concert with her sunglasses, she was relatively incognito. At least her bruise wasn't visible.

Then she made up for the lost time by mostly jogging until she got to the Algonquin's front desk and Jenna.

BAX LEFT DANNY'S TRAILER and headed straight back into the hotel. Danny's confession had filled in a whole lot of holes. While Bax had known Oscar was up to some bad crap, he'd never considered that Geiger and Oscar were partners. Oscar had manipulated all of their careers, slipped damaging photos to competing directors and producers so that his stars were trapped. He'd nearly destroyed Peter Eccles's life when the director had threatened to go to the papers.

But it was Nan's story that made the case. She'd been involved with the murder in Mexico, and there were photographs that would prove it. Only, Nan hadn't been the killer. Sure, she'd been stupid, but she hadn't been a murderer. It all came down to sex games gone bad. Danny didn't know if the girl who'd been killed had participated willingly, but it didn't matter. She hadn't signed up for death.

As Bax hit the garage entrance door, he listened to his messages from Mia, and then there was nothing else in his head. He speed dialed Mia. The phone rang twice before she picked up. Instead of hello, he heard, "Bax, thank God."

"What's wrong?"

"Did you get my calls?"

"I couldn't get back to you until now. What's going on? Why are you whispering? Where the hell are you?"

"Don't freak," she said.

"Too late."

"Listen—"

"Goddamn it, Mia."

"Listen!" she repeated. "I'm at 1560 Broadway near West 46th Street. Meet me here."

"What? Why?"

"Sheila Geiger is here. She's got a big suitcase with her. It's the pictures, Bax. All the pictures."

"Mia, stop. Do not follow her."

"I have to. If we lose the pictures, we lose all the evidence. I'm not going to let that happen."

"Ah, Jesus," he said, breaking out into a run to get to his car. "I don't give a damn about the pictures. So just stop, okay? Stop and come back here."

"She hasn't seen me. She won't. I need to find out where she's going."

"You do not. I'm charging Oscar. I've got him on blackmail this time, and it'll stick. He's going to tell us everything we need to know."

"That's wonderful, but— Wait."

He got to his car and as soon as he'd cranked the engine he stuck his light on top of the hood, then he was out of there, listening to her as she paid off her cabbie.

"Bax?"

"I'm almost there."

"She's going into the office building. I'm going to find out where she's headed."

"Mia, don't."

"She won't see me. I swear, Bax. You'll do all the heavy lifting."

"I swear to God, Mia, if something happens to you—"

"Nothing will."

"It can't. It really can't. This isn't going to end like that goddamn Nicholas Cage movie."

"What?" she asked.

He had to get to 5th Avenue to make the turn onto West 41st. Traffic made things difficult.

"Bax, what about Nicolas Cage?"

"You know that movie. With Meg Ryan. Nicolas Cage is the angel."

"Yeah, I remember."

"Oh, honey," she said, still whispering but her voice had gone all mushy. "I'm not going to get hit by a car."

"No, but you could get hit by a bullet."

"Bax, I'm in the building. I have to hang up now so I can get in the elevator. I'll call you the second I can. And Bax?"

"Yeah?"

"I love you, too."

The phone clicked off and Bax held back the urge to fling it into the windshield. The woman was insane. Stark raving mad. Not the good kind, either.

She should have stayed where she was safe. Even though he knew she would be careful, there was no way not to worry. If anything bad happened...

Shit. He really had gone and done it. Fallen in love with her. There was no use kidding himself about it. The die was cast. Him, who hadn't loved anyone his whole adult life. And he was all set to leave this city behind.

Only, he wasn't so sure any more. Because it wasn't just a city any more. It was her city.

Goddamn it.

THE BUILDING HAD TO BE forty stories high, which was a good thing in that there were lots and lots of people Mia could hide behind. But it also meant that she had to do some fancy footwork and a little shoving to get into the elevator with Sheila.

She kept her head down, her hat low. For comfort, she rubbed her fingers over her cell phone, knowing Bax was just on the other end. Even though the elevator was packed, it stopped three more times, and three more people shoved themselves in. Each time, Mia moved closer to Sheila until she was behind the woman. At the thirty-first floor, she disembarked and Mia realized not just where they were but why. Because they had arrived at the headquarters of the *National Tattler*.

BAX PARKED DAMN CLOSE to the entrance of the building.

The truck he blocked, well, that was just the driver's bad luck. He had to get to Mia, and he didn't care what it took. He got to the entrance and looked up. The building seemed as if it went on forever, that there were thousands of people swarming inside.

He looked at the cell in his hand, willing the damn thing to ring.

It was horrible, this feeling, as if he could quite literally tear his hair out in frustration. Nothing mattered except Mia's safety. Nothing.

The phone rang and it was at his ear in a split second. "Where are you?"

"Thirty-first floor," she said, still whispering. "The offices of the *National Tattler.*"

He'd bought a few copies of that one. It was particularly sensational, but the quality of the pages had been one of the best.

"Get out. Now that I know where she is, I'll take over."

"Uh, Bax? Don't freak."

He slammed his hand on the wall by the elevator. "What now?"

"Nan's here, too."

"And?"

"She's got a gun."

MIA REACHED BEHIND HER and sure enough, there was Carlane's hand to squeeze. The two of them were with eleven others, all of whom were standing by a long, low wall that divided the huge office. On one side there were a large group of desks, some of them with cubicles, some without, but all of them had computers.

Mia wasn't paying much attention to anything but Nan. And Nan's gun. She didn't look very stable. Not just because her gun hand was shaking, but because of the panic in her eyes.

Carlane wasn't much better. Mia could feel the terror in her friend, and there was no way of making it better. It was all her fault, all her stupidity. She'd brought Carlane straight into the middle of madness. If something happened to her, Mia would never forgive herself.

Unbelievably, it was Sheila who was holding Nan together, despite having had a number of cocktails at the Algonquin. She'd assessed the situation quickly and accurately. Her hands were in the air, and she was speaking slowly and carefully. "Nan, what are you doing? This isn't what we talked about."

"We didn't talk about you selling me out, either."

"Honey, you've got it all wrong."

Someone in Mia's group made a move, but Nan swung the gun toward the guy. Carlane gasped, and Mia stepped forward, blocking her friend.

"Don't you fucking move!" Nan shouted. "I'll shoot you as soon as look at you, got it?"

The guy, who was young and scared, put up his hands and slid back into the pack. They were all standing to the right of Sheila. There was an older man there, too, but it seemed to Mia that he was from the other side of the wall. Management. The people she was huddled with were younger. And more frightened.

Nan pulled the gun back toward Sheila. "You think I'm stupid."

It wasn't a question.

"Everyone always thinks I'm stupid. Well, I guess you're right, because out of all you disgusting leeches, I'm the one going down for this. You're the one who wanted Gerry murdered. You're the one who had the brilliant idea of shooting the concierge. You're so freakin' smart, that you figured you'd let me take the fall and you'd walk away with your money and your house and you wouldn't have to work a day in your life."

"I don't know what you're talking about."

"Too late, bitch. You think Oscar's the only one who knows how to tape conversations? You think Gerry's the only one who took pictures? I've got news for you. You're toast. You're history. You're not selling one picture of me, not one, you understand?"

The elevator dinged, and everyone turned. Including Nan. A heavyset woman walked out, saw the gun, then turned straight around and got back in the car.

Nan didn't miss a beat. She faced Sheila. "Give me that case, Sheila."

"We can work this out, Nan. There's enough for both of us. We'll make a fortune. You can finally get out from under that bastard's thumb. Isn't that what we said? Isn't that what you wanted? It can all happen now, if we just stay calm."

"How'd she find out about Mexico? Huh? What did you tell her?"

"Who, that girl from the hotel? It doesn't matter. She must have seen something about the film in one of the old articles, that's all."

"*That girl from the hotel?* Are you blind? Do you know who her boyfriend is?"

"What?"

"The cop, you idiot. That homicide detective is shagging that girl from the hotel. So now he knows about Mexico, too. But then, that's probably no surprise to you."

"Nan, come on. Look, if we leave now, before the police get here, we can make a deal. A good deal, okay? Nobody will go to jail. Nobody will ever know what happened in Mexico."

Nan was shaking now, and crying. She wiped her face with the back of her left hand, then put it back on the butt of the gun. "Oh, shut up. You think I would ever believe a word that came out of your mouth? Mexico is nothing compared to all this, and you know it."

She waved the gun around as if she didn't remember it was in her hand. Mia ducked along with her fellow hostages, and that's when she saw it. The woman next to her was holding her cell phone, pointing it toward Nan. The woman next to that woman was doing the same thing.

Mia turned and sure enough, everyone in the group had some kind of recording device in their hands. Were they crazy? Any second Nan Collins could jump off the deep end, and they were recording for the six-o'clock news? But then, that's what they did here, wasn't it? Record other people's pain? Their shame? They took delight in the capturing the worst of humanity, so why wouldn't they be enjoying this?

She didn't give a damn. All she wanted was to get Carlane out of there in one piece. She wanted Bax, and she wanted to be back in the hotel. She wanted to be in his arms, in his bed. No way she could die up here, right? Bax knew she was in trouble. Right this second he was probably outside the door, ready to swoop in and save the day.

"Mia," Carlane whispered, her voice trembling harder than her hand. "Please, I'm no good at this."

"He'll be here."

"When?"

"Any second. I promise."

"He has to be. I just can't stand this." Her terrified voice rose, and Mia tried to pull her down, but it was too late.

Nan turned on them, focusing on Carlane. "You can't stand this?" She walked toward them, her too-large gun pointing straight at Carlane. "You're just as much to blame as she is," Nan said, pointing back at Sheila. But then the gun returned. "You people make me sick. All you care about is your headlines, your sick pictures. The way you destroy lives, you think I have any qualms about destroying yours? I would be doing the world a favor to shoot every one of you."

Nan took another step forward and Carlane made a desperate sound. Mia had to act, and she had to do it now. She stood up, took her hat off. "You don't want her. She's nothing. She doesn't even work here."

Nan stared at her, and as recognition dawned, her face reddened. Mia prepared herself for the shot. She moved to the side, just enough that the bullet wouldn't pass through her and hit Carlane.

"What the fuck are you doing here?"

"I came to tell them," Mia said, pulling hope out of thin air, "that Oscar Weinberg's been arrested. For blackmail."

"What?"

Mia took a deep breath, then let go of Carlane's hand. She moved forward, closer to Nan. "We found all his tapes. All his memory cards. The police have everything they need to take him down. They're not after you, Nan. They know about Mexico, but there's nothing they can do about it. You're off the hook. It's all about Weinberg, not you."

"You're lying."

"Why else would I be here?"

Nan looked back at Sheila, who had put her hands down and was staring at Mia, just as confused as Nan to see her. Mia stole the opportunity to distance herself even further from Carlane and the others. "He's never going to get out of jail, Nan. They know it was a mistake, a tragedy, in Mexico. They also know that he's owned you ever since. You and Bobbi and Danny and even Peter Eccles. They know he set you all up. But they didn't have any evidence, and now they do. He can't talk his way out of this, or buy his way out. It's over."

"She's got pictures," Nan said, her voice quieter, but just as scared.

Mia looked at the man next to Sheila. "He'd be insane to run any pictures with the kind of lawsuit that's coming up. They'd be in court so fast it would make your head spin. The only pictures they're gonna run are the ones of Oscar Weinberg behind bars. And pretty soon, no one will even remember who Oscar Weinberg was."

Nan stared at her, and for a moment, Mia thought she'd done it. That she'd averted disaster and that Nan would drop the gun. But only for a moment.

The woman, her face still as red as her hair, turned to Sheila. "We know different, don't we, Sheila?"

"What do you mean?" Sheila no longer looked confused. In fact, for the first time, she seemed more terrified than Carlane. "Nan, I didn't—"

"Shut up, you bitch!" Nan screamed. "They've got me for murder. You knew they would. You planned this whole goddamn thing! You were there, in Mexico. You know I didn't kill that kid. Oscar did. The pervert wanted a young one, and he didn't want someone willing. So he got me to lure her into that back lot. Gave me the gun."

"I'll tell them Oscar killed her," Sheila said. "I swear."

"Yeah? You going to tell them he killed your husband? That he was the one in the parking garage?" Nan buckled, but only for a second. This time, when she raised the gun, it wasn't shaking at all. "Oscar Weinberg won't go to prison. He'll find a way to twist it, like he always does."

Mia stepped back. She'd tried, and failed, and if Bax didn't get here soon…

"Oh, Christ, I need to get out of here," Nan said, mostly to herself. "Give me the suitcase."

Sheila nodded. "Take it. But you're making a mistake. Without me, you're going down. Together, we can still make this work. I swear, Nan, you're not going to get a better offer."

"Not necessarily," the man next to Sheila said as he distanced himself from her. "I'm sure we could tell your story the way it should be told. With the right pictures and details, we might be able to hear the whole thing in, say,

Bali. Where they don't honor U.S. extraditions. No trial. No jail. You could live in paradise for the rest of your life."

Nan blinked and her hands began to waiver. "I don't believe you. None of you." She turned abruptly toward Mia and lurched forward. Mia tried to run, but Nan grabbed onto her arm. "You. You're my ticket out of here. You tell that boyfriend of yours I want a helicopter. I want money, enough to leave this fucking place. A plane. Got it? You tell him that."

"Why don't you tell me yourself?"

Mia spun around at Bax's voice, jerking herself out of Nan's grasp. He'd gotten there somehow without using the elevator, or at least this elevator. Now he stood with a clear shot at Nan, his weapon a whole lot steadier than hers, and no nonsense in his stare.

"Lower your weapon. Nice and slow."

Nan shook her head. "I'm not going to jail."

"Not my call, Nan. That'll be up to a judge and jury. But you are going to put that gun down because no one here's going to get hurt. There's a whole lot of police right outside these doors, Nan. Give it up. It's over."

"I'm not the one!" Nan screamed. "It's not my fault! I'm just the lackey. The one they call to do the dirty work."

She swung back until her gun was pointing at Sheila's chest. "She knows. She was part of it, and so was her husband. But Gerry, he was tired of dealing with her bullshit. Always drunk, always bitching at him. Ask her what the final straw was. Go ahead. Ask her."

"Nan, put the gun down and we'll ask her anything you like."

She just stepped closer to Sheila. "Tell them what happened, Sheila. You saw those pictures of Gerry with

Danny Austen, and it made you crazy. Gerry wasn't sleeping with you, so he had to be doing someone else. You figured I was screwing him, right? But that was okay because he sure as hell wasn't going to leave you for an extra. For a gofer."

Mia watched as Bax moved quietly and quickly in front of the group of hostages. He waved them back, and Mia helped usher them away from danger. Carlane first.

"But you saw those pictures of Gerry in Danny's bedroom, and that made you insane." Nan moved even closer to Sheila. In another second, the gun would touch Sheila's chest. "That was it, wasn't it? You wanted him dead for screwing Danny, but let me tell you something, Sheila. Gerry wasn't sleeping with anyone. He was just adding to Oscar's collection of pictures. Setting Danny up the way he set us all up. He didn't give a shit about Danny, or me, or you. All your husband cared about was the money."

Mia knew Bax would want her to leave, but she couldn't walk away. Not when he was still in danger. However, she did ease her way to the wall where Nan wouldn't have a shot at her.

"So you had him killed for nothing, you stupid bitch."

"I wasn't the one who killed him, was I? You were so desperate you would have done anything. But then, I knew that when I found out you were sleeping with Oscar."

"He made me!"

"Nobody made you do anything. You were easy, that's all. And too dumb to find your way out of a paper bag."

Nan had gone past livid to a trembling madness. She pushed the gun into Sheila's chest and Mia braced for the shot, but no shot came. Instead, Bax tackled Nan broadside and they both went slamming into the wall. Nan's gun hit the floor then spun under a table. Sheila fell to the floor as if all her bones had melted. And before Mia could even cry out, Bax was on his knees with Nan facedown. The handcuffs went on her as she wept like a child.

Mia closed her eyes as she thanked God that Bax was safe. That Carlane was safe. That it was finally over.

16

BAX WAS FINALLY FINISHED at the precinct. Oddly, he hadn't minded doing the paperwork, at least the part Grunwald couldn't cover, except that it kept him from where he wanted to be.

Mia was packing up the suite, getting ready to resume her life without murder and intrigue dogging her steps.

It wouldn't take him long to get to the hotel, where he'd speak to Piper, clear out his office, then join Mia in the suite.

He'd wanted Boulder as badly as he'd wanted anything in his life. That dream had kept him going, kept him putting one foot in front of the other despite his disappointments. He'd looked forward to school, to the environment, the exchange of ideas, the stimulation that had been missing for so many years. As for writing, yeah, he wasn't half bad. He had some online friends, people he'd never met in person but who'd become his sounding boards, his critique group, and they'd all been enthusiastic about his work. He knew at this point publication wasn't a pipe dream. It was within his grasp if he gave it the time and attention it deserved. He'd planned himself a good life, all right.

But the promise of a spectacular life beckoned.

Of course, nothing was set. Not yet. There were big

questions to ask and answer. Commitments to a way of life he'd never been good at. And then, there was Mia's path. Would it, could it, merge with his?

He pulled into the Hush garage, moving slowly past all the motor homes and production trucks. There were a few crew members milling about, but he knew that filming was stopped for the day. With the arrest of Oscar Weinberg, everything had ground to a halt. It was possible *Coming Soon* might never come at all, and that seemed right to Bax. The whole thing had been tainted by greed and blackmail, not to mention murder.

Sheila must be so pissed, knowing she'd had her husband killed for something he hadn't even done. Or maybe it didn't matter to her. Maybe she just had to have an excuse, any excuse, because taking responsibility for her own mistakes was simply too painful.

He'd heard of worse things, lots worse. For years he'd been shocked at people's reason for taking a life. But time and too many horrors had dulled his sense of outrage. He'd come to expect the worst in people instead of the best.

Until Mia.

He got out of the car and went into the hotel. It had become so familiar to him. He would never, on his own, have walked into this hotel, not even the bar or the restaurant. It wasn't his style. He preferred coffee shops and little out-of-the-way diners, but for a fancy-ass hotel, this place wasn't bad.

Piper had sure surprised him with her treatment of Mia. Most bosses would have sacked her on the spot, but Piper had seen the truth of her transgressions and looked to the future. She'd seen what an asset she had in Mia. How she added value to the hotel in a way that would translate not only in goodwill but in repeat business.

The staff he'd met had impressed him, too. He'd expected a bunch of snobs all vying for positions of power. What he'd found reminded him a lot of what he'd been looking forward to in Boulder—a convivial group of like-minded folks, all dedicated to achieving excellence. He wasn't naive enough to think every employee at Hush was great, but enough were to make a real impact.

In the borrowed office, he picked up the notepad he'd left there, then took great pleasure in dumping all those tabloids into the trash. That was it. He closed the door behind him and headed for the elevator.

He should go see Piper.

Piper could wait.

He hit the button for the 14th floor, as anxious as a kid at Christmas to see Mia. To celebrate their victory and to find out if his hopes could become a viable future.

He headed out quickly, but as he approached the suite his step faltered. It was quite possible he was way off base here. That Mia had been caught up in the drama of the case, not him. God, he hoped not.

He opened the door, and there she stood by the window. She turned when she heard him. Her smile lit up the room. "Bax," she said, as she came toward him. The scar on her temple still made him ache, made him sorry he'd been so easy on Nan.

He pulled Mia into his arms and forgot about everything but the pleasure of holding this woman. He kissed her, and it was the closest thing to home he'd felt in years. She still smelled like flowers, like happiness. Just holding her made him feel absurdly lucky, as if he'd won all the lotteries there were.

As the sun spilled into the room and the clock ticked

away, he kept on kissing her, and she kept on kissing him back. There was desperation in her hands though, as she threaded her fingers through his hair.

As difficult as it was, he pulled back. "Hey," he said, looking into her amazing eyes. "We should talk."

She nodded, then she stepped away. "I guess it really is over," she said.

"There'll be more. Probably a trial. A deposition for you, I would imagine. Lots of paperwork for me."

"You mean for Grunwald," she said, giving him a quick glance before getting busy with the laptop.

He walked over to the couch and sat, then patted the seat next to him. "Come on. Let's talk."

She came to him slowly. The look on her face made him wonder if she was dreading what she was about to hear, or what she was about to say. Maybe it would be easier on both of them if he just said what he wanted. Yeah. That would be the exact right thing to do, if only he could remember how to talk.

Mia watched the color drain from Bax's face and her chest squeezed so hard she had to force the next breath. She touched his knee, grounding herself in the sturdy feel of him. He might be leaving, but not today. There was time enough to be depressed when he was actually in Boulder.

"Here's the deal," he said. "I—" He closed his mouth, shook his head, then looked at her again, this time square in the eyes. "I'm in love with you."

As wonderful as it was to hear, his words weren't exactly what she was hoping to hear. Not that she wasn't over the moon that he loved her, but she kind of knew that already. She wanted to know what he planned to do about it.

"You've changed things," he said. "Changed me.

Despite the fact that I'd be willing to walk on hot coals to keep you from getting hurt, this was the most satisfying case of my career. Not because I solved it, but because we solved it."

"We did?"

Bax put his hand on her neck as if he meant to pull her into a kiss, but he didn't. He just kept looking into her eyes. "It's crazy. Working with you was everything I'd wanted when I first joined the force. I had this totally idealized version of what being a cop would be. It was based on fiction. Literally. I'd read so many detective stories, from Cadfael to Spenser to Poirot, and all of them had someone they could talk to, someone with a sharp mind, a quick wit, who volleyed ideas like Wimbledon champions until the case was solved, the bad guys thwarted. I was, let's just say, disabused of that notion quickly. Painfully. I had to leave because every day I walked through the valley of my broken, childish dreams. And then you came along."

Mia was practically swooning at his words. "I'm your Beringar? Your Susan Silverman? Your…damn, who was with Poirot?"

"Captain Hastings," he said, grinning.

"Because you know what?"

"What?"

"I'm in love with you, too. And I loved working with you on this case so much, I can't even find words."

"Good, because I'm not finished."

"Oh," she said, closing her mouth. Dying to hear the rest.

"We're good together, you and I," he said. "I think that was my point. Not just when there's a case to solve, either. I haven't looked forward to anyone, ever, the way I look forward to you. So, depending on, well, you, I'm not going to Boulder."

Mia took in a deep draught of air because she had to be mature here, not just selfish. "What about the Ph.D? Teaching? Writing?"

"The doctorate was never the real point. That was just to have some leverage in teaching. The writing, I can still do. It may not be under a big tree in a national forest, but who cares."

"And the teaching?"

He touched the side of her face. "Teaching was just another way of searching for what's been missing. And wouldn't you know? The thing I was missing was you."

Mia wanted to fall into his arms and never, ever come up for air, but there were still things to be said. Asked. "Here's what's scary for me. I love the idea of being your companion, your partner, whatever you want to call it, but I don't want to be responsible for your happiness. Just as I wouldn't expect you to be responsible for mine. Do you really think we're enough to make you happy being a detective? The paperwork is still going to be there. So are all the other things that made you want to leave."

"God, this makes me love you even more. I've thought about it a lot. There's a magic here, between us, that extends beyond the bedroom. I'm not making that up, am I?"

"No, you're not."

"I never would have put it together, how great a team a concierge and a homicide cop could be. But we are. I don't think I'll be taking too much from you. I know you love your job, and I want nothing more than to support that. But you have to tell me if you don't want to play."

"I do. More than you can imagine. I want to play. I want

us to get our own whiteboard. I want to bug Miguel and Grunwald. I want to hear all the details, and I'm even willing to look at the icky pictures. Because there is nothing cooler in the whole world than you and me, working it together."

He sighed. "Sure now? There's still time to back out. Boulder's not going anywhere. I can always turn to Plan B."

"I'm sure. I want to give this a go, Bax. With everything I've got."

"Thank God. I think I would have wept like a schoolgirl if you'd said anything else."

She stood, but only long enough to climb into his lap, to wrap her legs around him and lock her arms around his neck. "Who'd have thunk, huh? The concierge and the detective. Kinda sounds like the beginning of a beautiful partnership. Or maybe a big feature film?"

"No more movies, please. I've had enough of those for a while. But the partnership? Oh, yeah. I can see that having a very extended run."

She leaned that little bit forward until her lips brushed his. "I don't think the boss would mind if we stayed one more night in this suite."

"Especially if we don't ask," he said. Then he kissed her. And it was perfect.

* * * * *

*Look for another exciting Blaze story set
at the fabulous Hush hotel.
HAVE MERCY by Jo Leigh,
featuring pet concierge Mercy Jones,
is on sale in May 2008. Enjoy!*

Enjoy a sneak preview of
MATCHMAKING WITH A MISSION
by B.J. Daniels,
part of the **WHITEHORSE, MONTANA** *miniseries.*
Available from Harlequin Intrigue
in April 2008.

Nate Dempsey has returned to Whitehorse to uncover the truth about his past...

Nate sensed someone watching the house and looked out in surprise to see a woman astride a paint horse just on the other side of the fence. He quickly stepped back from the filthy second-floor window, although he doubted she could have seen him. Only a little of the June sun pierced the dirty glass to glow on the dust-coated floor at his feet as he waited a few heartbeats before he looked out again.

The place was so isolated he hadn't expected to see another soul. Like the front yard, the dirt road was waist-high with weeds. When he'd broken the lock on the back door, he'd had to kick aside a pile of rotten leaves that had blown in from last fall.

As he sneaked a look, he saw that she was still there, staring at the house in a way that unnerved him. He shielded his eyes from the glare of the sun off the dirty window and studied her, taking in her head of long blond hair that feathered out in the breeze from under her Western straw hat.

She wore a tan canvas jacket, jeans and boots. But it was

the way she sat astride the brown-and-white horse that nudged the memory.

He felt a chill as he realized he'd seen her before. In that very spot. She'd been just a kid then. A kid on a pretty paint horse. Not this one—the markings were different. Anyway, it couldn't have been the same horse, considering the last time he had seen her was more than twenty years ago. That horse would be dead by now.

His mind argued it probably wasn't even the same girl. But he knew better. It was the way she sat the horse, so at home in a saddle and secure in her world on the other side of that fence.

To the boy he'd been, she and her horse had represented freedom, a freedom he'd known he would never have— even after he escaped this house.

Nate saw her shift in the saddle, and for a moment he feared she planned to dismount and come toward the house. With Ellis Harper in his grave, there would be little to keep her away.

To his relief, she reined her horse around and rode back the way she'd come.

As he watched her ride away, he thought about the way she'd stared at the house—today and years ago. While the smartest thing she could do was to stay clear of this house, he had a feeling she'd be back.

Finding out her name should prove easy, since he figured she must live close by. As for her interest in Harper House… He would just have to make sure it didn't become a problem.

* * * * *

Be sure to look for
MATCHMAKING WITH A MISSION
and other suspenseful Harlequin Intrigue stories,
available in April
wherever books are sold.

n o c t u r n e™

The Bloodrunners
trilogy continues with book #2.

The hunt meant more to Jeremy Burns than dominance—
it meant facing the woman he left behind. Once
Jillian Murphy had belonged to Jeremy, but now she was
the Spirit Walker to the Silvercrest wolves. It would take
more than the rights of nature for Jeremy to renew his
claim on her—and she would not go easily once he had.

LAST WOLF HUNTING

by RHYANNON BYRD

Available in April wherever books are sold.

Be sure to watch out for the last book,
Last Wolf Watching, available in May.

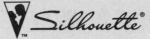
Romantic
SUSPENSE

**Sparked by Danger,
Fueled by Passion.**

The Taken

Tierney Doyle is used to being criticized for
her psychic abilities, yet the tough-as-nails—
and drop-dead-gorgeous—detective has no doubt
about what she has uncovered in the case of a
string of unsolved murders. And Tierney is slowly
discovering that working so close to her partner,
detective Wade Callahan, could be lethal.

Look for

Danger Signals
by Kathleen Creighton

Available in April wherever books are sold.

introduces...

Lust in Translation
A sexy new international miniseries.

Don't miss the first book...

FRENCH KISSING
by Nancy Warren

April 2008

N.Y. fashionista Kimi Renton knows sexy
photographer Holden McGregor is a
walking fashion disaster. And she's tried
to make him over. But when they're
lip-locked, it's ooh-la-la all the way!

LUST IN TRANSLATION

Because sex is the same
in any language!

HB79393

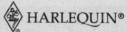

HARLEQUIN®

Blaze™

COMING NEXT MONTH

#387 ONE FOR THE ROAD Crystal Green
Forbidden Fantasies

A cross-country trek. A reckless sexual encounter. Months ago, Lucy Christie wouldn't have considered either one a possibility. But now she is on the road, looking for thrills, adventure...sex. And the hot cowboy Lucy meets on the way seems just the man for the job....

#388 SEX, STRAIGHT UP Kathleen O'Reilly
Those Sexy O'Sullivans, Bk. 2

It's all on the line when Catherine Montefiore's family legacy is hit by a very public scandal. In private, she's hoping hot Irish hunk Daniel O'Sullivan can save the day. He's got all the necessary skills and, straight up or not, Catherine will have a long drink of Daniel any way she can get him....

#389 FRENCH KISSING Nancy Warren
Lust in Translation

New York fashionista Kimi Renton *knows* sexy photographer Holden McGregor is a walking fashion disaster. And she's tried to make him over. But when they're lip-locked it's *ooh la-la* all the way!

#390 DROP DEAD GORGEOUS Kimberly Raye
Love at First Bite, Bk. 2

Dillon Cash used to be the biggest geek in Skull Creek, Texas—until a vampire encounter changed him into a lean, mean sex machine. Now every woman in town wants a piece of the hunky cowboy. Every woman, that is, except his best friend, Meg Sweeney. But he'll convince her....

#391 NO STOPPING NOW Dawn Atkins

A gig as cameraperson on Doctor Nite's cable show is a coup for Jillian James and her documentary on bad-for-you bachelors. But behind the scenes, Brody Donegan is sexier than she expected. How can she get her footage if she can't keep out of his bed?

#392 PUTTING IT TO THE TEST Lori Borrill
Blush

Matt Jacobs is the man to beat—and Carly Abrams is determined to do what it takes to outsmart him on a matchmaking survey—even cheat. But Carly's problems don't *really* start until Matt—the star of her nighttime fantasies—wants to put her answers to the test!

www.eHarlequin.com

HBCNM0308